Pucker Up

Sweet Pickle Books
47 Orchard Street
New York, NY 10002

ALSO BY RHONDA STAPLETON

Stupid Cupid

Flirting with Disaster

Pucker Up

Rhonda Stapleton

SIMON PULSE
New York   London   Toronto   Sydney

SIMON PULSE
An imprint of Simon & Schuster Children's Publishing Division
1230 Avenue of the Americas, New York, NY 10020
First Simon Pulse edition May 2010
Copyright © 2010 by Rhonda Stapleton
All rights reserved, including the right of reproduction in whole or in part in any form.
SIMON PULSE and colophon are registered trademarks of Simon & Schuster, Inc.
For information about special discounts for bulk purchases, please contact
Simon & Schuster Special Sales at 1-866-506-1949 or business@simonandschuster.com.
The Simon & Schuster Speakers Bureau can bring authors to your live event. For more
information or to book an event contact the Simon & Schuster Speakers Bureau
at 1-866-248-3049 or visit our website at www.simonspeakers.com.
Designed by Michael Rosamilia
The text of this book was set in Adobe Caslon Pro.
Manufactured in the United States of America
2 4 6 8 10 9 7 5 3 1
Library of Congress Control Number 2009938356
ISBN 978-1-4169-7466-6
ISBN 978-1-4424-0642-1 (eBook)

I'd like to dedicate this book to all of those magical things

that kept me alive while writing and editing this trilogy: awesome

family, supportive friends, superfunny work buddies, booty-shaking

music, chocolate, General Tso's chicken, back massages, copious

amounts of caffeine, late-night brainstorming sessions, sunny days at

Panera, comfy pajama bottoms, the microwave, my awesome laptop,

sushi, caramel macchiatos at Starbucks, and the veritable cornucopia

of scribbled papers and sticky notes plastered all over my house.

Chapter 1

Could a person die of happiness overload? Because if that were possible, I was so going to keel over any second.

But what a way to go.

My brand-new boyfriend Derek's strong, lean fingers threaded tightly through mine as we strolled through the door of Starbucks. It was our first official date since we'd begun going out yesterday afternoon. We'd decided to grab some coffee after school to discuss how to help all the broken-hearted single people I'd hastily matched with each other when I was trying to reverse the effects of me accidentally making them all fall in love with him.

Yeah, not one of the better ideas I've had in the couple of months since being hired by my boss, Janet, at Cupid's Hollow.

But fortunately for me, I also found out yesterday that Derek was a fellow cupid, and he'd promised to help me out. And I just knew that we were going to make things right—together.

"Hey, Felicity, what kind of drink do you want?" he asked, turning those piercing green eyes to me.

I swallowed, wanting to pinch myself in über-glee. I was on an honest-to-God date with the guy I'd been crushing on since freshman year, something I'd fantasized about for*ever*.

"Felicity?" he asked, one eyebrow raised.

Hey, dork! He asked you a question! I mentally chided myself, trying to snap out of my love haze.

"Um, how about a Mocha Frappuccino?" I suggested. "Those are supergood." And super laden with caffeine. Yum!

He smiled, his cheek dimpling slightly. "Sure. Why don't you find us a private spot to sit?"

I nodded, picking out a booth in the back corner where no one was around and settling into one side of the table. Plenty of isolation for us to discuss our top secret cupid business matters.

Digging through my purse, I pulled out my hot-pink LoveLine 3000, the handheld technology we cupids use to send matchmaking e-mails to our targets. I put it on my lap, turning it on.

While I waited for Derek to return, I kept myself occupied by staring at his absolutely perfect butt.

After a couple of minutes Derek sauntered over to the table, drinks in hand, and slid into the booth seat across from me. I accepted my drink gratefully and forced myself to take a slow sip through the straw, not wanting to give myself brain freeze. That crap *hurt*.

"Okay, I'm dying to ask you a question," I finally said, leaning over the table toward Derek in excitement. "When Janet hired you, did she take you to the bow-and-arrow room and give you a . . . demonstration?"

I rubbed the middle of my chest, remembering how it had felt at my interview to have the gold arrow hit me and disappear, leaving only a tingle. Janet, our boss, sure didn't mess around . . . she'd wanted to make sure I knew the cupid powers were real. Not that I'd doubted her after she shot me, but over time I'd learned the reality of matchmaking all too well . . . both the ups and downs.

Derek laughed. "So she shot you with an arrow also. Glad I wasn't the only doubter she'd hired."

God, it was so awesome to be able to work with my new boyfriend. I'd finally have someone I could talk about my cupid woes with! Not that I wasn't desperate to dish it all to my two best friends, Andy and Maya . . . but my contract specifically stipulated I wasn't allowed to tell anyone the specifics of my job, upon pain of death.

Okay, the contract terms weren't *that* drastic, but I just knew something awful *would* happen to me. I sure didn't want to find out what, though.

"Janet's kind of scary," I whispered, almost afraid that by some weird voodoo she could overhear me talking about her.

"No kidding. She's intimidating." He took the lid off his cup, releasing a puff of steam into the air, and took a drink.

"So, how many matches have you made so far?" I asked him. We each had a weekly quota to meet, and I was eager for tips and motivation.

"Only a few." He shrugged. "I'm trying to take my time and still perfect my profiles. It's hard work, studying everyone and making sure I represent them accurately."

I nodded in sympathy. "Yeah, it took me a while to do those too."

A souring thought hit me, and I pinched my lips together. If I'd taken more time to add greater details to my profiles, like Derek was doing, maybe I wouldn't have made so many bad matches since I'd started working as a cupid. And thus, there wouldn't be so many desolate people grumping their way through school when their love spells had worn off.

Shaking my head resolutely, I pushed the thought out of my brain. All I'd been trying to do was get my classmates' attention off Derek and back on one another, where it belonged. Besides, there were now two matchmakers on the job at Greenville High, ready and eager to get things fixed up before prom, which would be in just over three weeks.

And I couldn't focus on my own prom happiness with Derek until I got these disaster matches resolved, once and for all.

I took my LoveLine 3000 out of my lap and put it on the table-top, ready to get down to business. "Did you bring yours?"

"Sure did." Derek tugged his out of his back pocket and turned it on. "Last night I made a list of everyone in school who is currently single and in need of a match. I'll e-mail you half of the list." He bent his head over the PDA, typing on the little keyboard.

Weird, I'd never thought about e-mailing another cupid. I wonder what would happen when he sent me the document. Would it make us fall even more in love? Maybe we would be like my parents were when I'd had a "brilliant" idea and decided to matchmake the two of them for their anniversary a few weeks ago.

I shuddered, remembering their feet sticking out of their bedroom doorway as they went at it on their floor. Time to push that gross little memory into the dark recesses of my brain, back where it belonged.

"Hey, you still here?" Derek asked, a crooked grin on his face. He reached over and brushed my hand, causing my skin to tingle.

"Yeah, sorry, had a bad flashback," I said, drinking some of my Frappuccino with my free hand. I'd tell him about matchmaking my parents later, after I'd done another mental scrub or two or twenty.

My PDA vibrated. I opened my new e-mail from Derek, half expecting my chest to tingle—the surefire identifier of a love match.

Nothing happened.

After staring dumbly at the screen for several long seconds, I almost smacked my own forehead. *Duh, Felicity.* I'd forgotten that cupids can't matchmake themselves, so Derek sending me an e-mail wouldn't have any power over me, anyway.

I focused my attention on the list, scrolling down to check out the names. "Okay, I need to make matches for everyone on here, right?"

"Yeah. I think if we take our time and do some quality matches, they should hold together with better odds."

My stomach twitched. He was right, of course, but I was embarrassed that Derek, who had been a cupid for only a few weeks, had managed to figure out more about matchmaking than I had.

He reached back into his pocket and pulled out his cupid manual. "Each person can be matched with someone else on the list, just to keep things simple. I prepared the two lists according to the manual. There was one formula that seemed overly complicated, but the one on page"—he drawled off, flipping through the book—"fifty-two seemed like it would do the job."

Derek turned the manual facing toward me and pointed at a tiny chart filled with wavy lines and arrows.

Yeahhhhh . . . I'd completely forgotten about that book. Whoops. The writing was so dry and boring, I'd almost fallen asleep reading it. I think I'd stuffed it in my bookshelf a few days after becoming a cupid and never opened it up again, preferring to wing it my own way.

I nodded sagely, pretending I could interpret the chart. "Good thinking. That one should work out great." Right, like I knew what the crap he was talking about.

I made a mental note to dig my manual out again and make a more valiant effort to read the damn thing. Geez, we'd only been here a short time, and already Derek was schooling me in the art and science of matchmaking. How mortifying.

My cheeks burned.

Well, it was my own fault. This wasn't the time for embarrassment or shame. I had to do what the situation called for, and none of my ideas had worked out well so far. Time to try Derek's plan now.

"Let's run this by Janet first," I said, "just to be safe." I knew from experience that our boss liked to be kept in the loop. Plus, she'd probably like to see us working together. And anything that made Janet happy was good in my book.

"Sure, that's a good idea." He took a sip of his drink and smiled at me. "I'm looking forward to working with you."

"Me too," I replied with a happy sigh, a warm glow spreading through my chest and limbs.

I didn't need a love arrow shot at me to make me get tingles— being in Derek's presence was more than enough.

"Well," Janet said to me and Derek, leaning back in her plush executive chair, "I think that's a great plan. And I like even more how you two are working together on this. I was hoping you'd get along." She gave us a nod of approval.

I beamed, happy that Janet could not only squeeze in a meeting with us on such short notice but also approved of our idea on how to fix the matchmaking mess at school. That way we could get started on it ASAP.

"Thanks," I replied, excitement bubbling in my voice. "Derek's great to work with." With all the strength I could muster, I resisted the urge to cast a lovey-dovey gaze at Derek, who was sitting in the chair beside me, across from Janet's desk. But out of the corner of my eye, I saw him smile at my words.

After solidifying our matchmaking plan at Starbucks earlier today, Derek and I had also decided we'd lie low with the boyfriend/girlfriend stuff around work until we'd scoped the situation out first. Janet didn't know we were dating, and we didn't want to make anything more complicated than necessary right now.

"Okay, let me see your PDAs," she said, reaching her hands out toward us. "I'll download a copy of your lists for reference."

We handed them over to her, and she synced them, one by one, to her main computer. After she was done, she laid them on the desk. "I'll review the documents later, but it seems like you're on the right track." She paused. "Actually, Derek, since you're here, there's another guy cupid I'd like to introduce you to. He's in the office next door. Felicity, we'll be back in a few minutes—just wait right here."

"Sure thing," I said, trying not to give Derek any inappropriately slutty looks as he filed past me and followed Janet out the door.

I crossed my legs and fidgeted for a couple of minutes. Then I stood up and plucked my PDA off her desk so I could put it back in my purse. As I lifted the LoveLine 3000, I saw my name at the top of a list on the left page of her daily planner. My heart pounded, and I swallowed hard.

Was I in trouble? Maybe she was on to me and Derek and was upset about us dating. Or maybe she'd found out some of my other cupid secrets, like that I'd previously matchmade my friend Maya with three guys ... or that I'd paired up my parents for their anniversary. I'd deleted those e-mails from my LoveLine 3000, but maybe she'd gotten the info somehow.

I had to know. With a furtive glance at the door, I quickly jerked the planner off the desk, scanning its contents. It was a to-do list, and there was a checkbox beside me. And after my name was Derek's name. Under us were other pairs of names. What was this?

Then it hit me.

Janet must have matchmade me and Derek.

Chapter 2

My jaw dropped in shock. Janet had paired us up? But I didn't remember getting a love e-mail or anything else yesterday. In fact, I didn't remember any sort of weird tingling feeling at all.

I shook my head, staring at the words. How had she done it?

Well, cupids *have* been around for thousands of years. Maybe there were many other methods of matchmaking that I hadn't even imagined.

The doorknob turned. I dropped the planner, deftly plopping back in my seat. Something told me I probably wasn't supposed to know about being matchmade, so I decided to keep my mouth shut about what I'd seen.

"You can call him anytime," Janet said to Derek as they walked into the room. "Okay, we're all done here, you two." She moved behind her desk and handed Derek his PDA back. "I'll see you in your individual meetings next week."

He turned and smiled at me, his eyes lighting up as they crinkled in the corners. I melted a little, like ooey-gooey butter. If he and I were together a hundred years, I'd never get enough of him.

Then a startling thought flew into my mind. Did this new discovery of mine mean the only reason Derek was in love with me was because we'd been paired together by Janet? Was his love genuine or just a result of a magically induced spell? I knew mine was sincere because I'd been in love with him for years. But it wasn't the same story for Derek.

With suddenly shaky legs I stood, offering Janet a weak smile. "Well, I'd better get home before my mom wonders where her car is."

We headed back to the parking lot. I tucked my hand into Derek's, but on the inside I was almost dizzy from the new worry that swirled in my head. I knew I should be more understanding of Janet's actions. After all, that's what *I* did for a living—find people who belong together and give them a chance at love. But I had to admit, I'd never considered the idea that Derek and I could have been paired up too.

I guess I'd just figured that he and I were destined to be together and that my bold confession to him in the cafeteria yesterday about my true feelings had set our destiny into motion. I still couldn't believe I'd found the courage to spill my guts in front of Derek, his friends, and a crapload of people eating lunch, me loudly proclaiming that I'd been crushing on him since freshman year. Even now my stomach flipped over itself when I thought of it.

We stopped at Derek's car. He tugged me close to him, and I reveled in the sensation of his warm body against mine.

He pressed his lips on the top of my head. "I'll give you a call tonight," he whispered against my hair.

I nodded, not trusting myself to speak. He got into his car and waved as he drove away from me.

After slipping into my own driver's seat, I navigated out of the parking lot and through the back ways to get home, unable to enjoy the usual pleasure I got from seeing the springtime blossoms erupting on the trees lining the streets of the neighborhoods. As I drove, I wrestled back and forth with the idea of letting Derek know we'd been paired up, then decided against it. I didn't want to plant any seeds of doubt in Derek's mind about what I now perceived as our fragile relationship.

Now I almost wished I *hadn't* seen Janet's planner because I was going to be superparanoid and would scrutinize every aspect of our relationship for the next two weeks. Especially since I knew from professional experience that, unfortunately, pairing two people didn't mean they'd stay together after the love spell wore off.

I pulled the car into the driveway and ambled into my house. Though I was tempted to run straight to the freezer and grab a carton of Chunky Monkey ice cream for insta-therapy, I was better off trying to push my worried thoughts out of my head and make some love matches instead.

If I continued eating ice cream every time I was upset, I was gonna have to wear a muumuu to prom. And there was no way I was going to eat myself right out of my fabulously hot red dress.

"Mom, I'm home from my work meeting," I said, dropping the borrowed keys back on top of her purse on the hall table. I gazed at the logo on the car key chain and sighed. How many lasting love matches would I have to make to save up for a car of my own? It sure would be nice to start getting more bonuses in my paycheck.

"Hey, Felicity," she said from the kitchen table. "Did you put the car keys back in my purse?"

I resisted the urge to roll my eyes at the House Nazi. "Yes, *Mom*, I did."

I flew up the stairs toward my room.

"Make sure you clean up that mess in your room," Mom yelled up to me.

Sheesh. I closed my door and grabbed my phone off my side table. I was desperate to call someone and talk about Derek, but I didn't want to be one of those obnoxious chicks who did nothing but blab on and on and on about her boyfriend. Ick. That got old fast.

Instead, I dialed one of my BFFs, Andy, to see what she was up to.

"Hey, Felicity," she said when she picked up. "Long time, no talkee. I'm still cracking up about your cafeteria love confession yesterday. I only wish I'd been there to witness it."

"Yeah, I think I'm a legend at school now," I said, giggling. I thought school today would have been a nightmare of one embarrassment after another, given the way I'd practically screamed my love for Derek out loud. But instead, I'd had several girls come up to me and congratulate me on being so ballsy, wishing they had the guts to do the same thing with the guys they liked.

And Mallory, the über-jerk who had started the whole incident by threatening to rat my feelings out to Derek in front of everyone, had stayed away from me all day today. Talk about an unexpected bonus!

On the other end of the phone I heard Andy's mom hollering something at her.

"Okay!" Andy said to her, her voice piercing my eardrums. "Sorry, I gotta go," she mumbled to me. "Mom asked me to run up to the store and pick her up another container of soy milk." She sighed. "I'm so, soooo glad I got my license. I always wanted to be her personal errand girl."

"You're not the only one," I commiserated. "Mom seems to think I'll jump at the chance to borrow the car, even if it's picking up her crap." After saying that, I peeked toward the door, half-afraid the House Nazi had somehow overheard my griping. She had a way of knowing everything that happened in this house.

"We'll catch up tomorrow, 'kay?"

"Sure thing," I said. "Have fun."

We hung up.

I sludged over to my bookshelf. Guilt over my lazy cupidness forced me to pull out the manual Janet had given me when I was hired. Draping across my bed, I tucked a pillow under my upper body and flipped the book open to the description of the chart Derek had pointed out. Surely the guidebook wasn't as bad as I remembered.

After all, if Derek could get it, so could I, right?

I'd heard in my health class that after childbirth women somehow mentally block how painful the whole birthing process was. My teacher had explained that was nature's way of making sure people continued to have kids instead of just popping out one and then never having another baby again because of all the pain.

Maybe being a cupid came with the same kind of mystical amnesia because after staring at that stupid chart in the manual, I'd quickly realized that I'd forgotten how wretched that book was. And how painful it was to be going through it again, especially when the material read like this:

> To facilitate the highest-quality compatibility between
> two parties, refer to chart 412B, above. Note: The
> applied elements contained within the chart, combined
> with a timely and accurate profile for each party, will

ensure a higher ratio of matchmaking accuracy,

provided all conditions are met.

I'd studied that one page for a full half hour, finally succumbing to my impulse to close the book and throw it back onto my bookshelf, where it would meet its final resting place.

Maybe I was better off just talking to Derek if I had questions. That way I would encourage conversation between us . . . which would allow me to take some notes as I shamelessly picked his brain. Plus, it would help get my mind off the whole love-spell thing between us, which was now constantly lurking in the back of my consciousness.

The evening had passed fast. I'd made a few matches from my list and had gone to bed early, eager to start seeing the results. Especially since I'd noticed, as I headed toward school this morning, that many students were still sour and depressed. People shuffled quietly through the hallways, grousing under their breaths.

It would be so easy to sink back into a deep funk and let it get me down too, but I was determined to float above it.

"Hey," Maya called out to me, waving with her free hand. In the other hand she clutched her ever-present trumpet case.

I gave her a quick hug. "How's it going?"

She shrugged. "Not bad. Except—"

Before she could finish, Scott, her supercutie boyfriend, came up and gave her a big hug from behind, kissing the top of her head.

I smiled, warmed by my friend's romantic happiness . . . and, to be honest, by the fact that this was a match I'd made that had actually lasted.

Maya turned to face him, hugging tightly. "Hey, you."

The first bell rang. I glanced around but didn't see Andy. I wasn't alarmed, though—she sometimes ran on her own schedule, and I knew she'd check in with us soon enough.

Maya and I said good-bye to Scott, then went to our first period English class. Mrs. Kendel was at her usual station by the door.

"Miss Takahashi, Miss Walker, come in," she said gruffly, waving us in with her thick hand. She closed the door after we entered and went to the chalkboard, writing some terms on the board.

I slid into my seat and, with as much subtlety as I could, glanced over at Mike, a quiet guy in the back corner of our classroom. He was one of the people I'd matchmade last night after studying the list carefully to find the perfect person for him.

I'd finally settled on Adele, the girl who was assigned the seat in front of him. She was usually a quiet person as well, and they seemed to be nicely suited for each other. I'd even used more than my usual three compatibility factors, just to make sure they had enough in common to make the match last.

Plus, I had no doubt that Mike was already crushing on her. Throughout the year I'd seen him look at Adele when he thought she wasn't looking. I hadn't paired them up before because she'd had a boyfriend, but they'd broken up recently.

And no, that *wasn't* my fault, thank you very much—they had been together before I'd become a cupid.

Now that she was single, and happened to be on my list, she was fair game.

Adele hadn't arrived in class yet, and I couldn't read Mike's face to see if he'd opened the love e-mail I'd sent him. He was as calm and serene as ever.

I chewed on my lower lip, hoping I hadn't messed up. He wasn't exuding any kind of romantic aura around him, and most guys by now were practically—

Right then Adele slipped into the room, instantly casting her gaze onto Mike.

He rose from his seat, going right to her.

"Mr. Jones," Mrs. Kendel said, her wrinkled face scrunched up in irritation. "Please take your seat."

Ignoring the teacher, he and Adele leaped into each other's arms, boldly kissing right there in class.

My eyes about popped out of my head, and I cupped my hand over my mouth in surprise. I guess it was the quiet ones you had to watch out for. Well, at least I had solid confirmation that the matchmaking had worked.

The class erupted in equal parts applause and giggles. Even in a negative mood, no one could resist people publicly proclaiming their horniness in the middle of class. Some things never change.

"You go, girl!" one girl cried out.

"Get it on!" a guy in the back of class said, chortling wildly.

"Mr. Jones! Miss Mossinger!" Mrs. Kendel snapped, stepping over to the two of them and tugging them apart with a hefty jerk.

Mike's and Adele's lips made a popping sound from being separated so quickly, and they stared at each other with glazed eyes. Mike's mouth was smeared all over with Adele's pastel-pink lipstick.

"Need I remind you that this is *not* appropriate behavior in class?" Mrs. Kendel sniffed in disdain, anger making her body shake. "Go to the principal's office, *now!*"

A few students snickered as Mike and Adele walked out of the classroom hand in hand, oblivious to Mrs. Kendel's blast. She stared in shock at their retreating figures and gripped the end of the door, forgetting for the moment that she was supposed to be teaching us about whatever crap she'd been in the middle of writing on the board.

"You know they're going to the bleachers," some smart-ass guy behind me said quietly. "They're so gonna make a baby."

Maya snorted. "Holy crap, was that crazy," she said.

"Just as crazy as when that one photography guy came in here and read you that poem," a girl on the other side of her whispered, loud enough for everyone to hear. "Remember that? God, that was awesome," she said wistfully.

Maya's cheeks flamed red, and she cast her gaze onto her desk.

I'd completely forgotten about Quentin, one of the three guys I'd initially paired Maya with in my fiasco-fest back in March. He'd burst into the classroom and had begged Mrs. Kendel to let him ask Maya out on a date via his lame poem. And I was willing to bet Maya had probably blocked that little memory as well.

"Anyway," I said, trying to change the subject and save Maya the embarrassment of dates from the past, "aren't you glad we're finally done with reading novels in here and are moving on to something different?"

At my words, Mrs. Kendel finally shook herself out of her shock and shuffled over to the chalkboard. I guess I couldn't blame her—she'd been a teacher here forever and a day and probably had never had things like this happen until I became a cupid. The poor woman was going to be driven to early retirement if her students didn't knock it off with the crazy makey-outey stuff.

It also didn't help things that pairing her up with the chemistry teacher last month during my frantic rematching had ended disastrously. I'd seen last night that she was on my list of people to fix, but I had *no* idea what kind of a man was right for her. Which meant I needed to watch her closely and get to know her better.

A fun prospect for me. This one would require all the magic I could scrounge up in my PDA.

Mrs. Kendel shook her head rapidly and blinked. Then she turned a beady eye toward the class, clearing her throat. "Class," she said in a crisp, professional voice, as if the last couple of minutes never happened, "we're going to be discussing narratives for the next couple of weeks. We'll start by reading examples of stellar narratives and then follow the lesson up by writing a narrative of our own." Before anyone could respond, she continued, "And, yes, before you ask, it will be graded."

I groaned inwardly, rolling my eyes in Maya's direction. She suppressed a giggle in response.

We both knew what this meant. What should probably have been a relatively fun project would most likely have all the life sucked out of it by Mrs. Kendel, in the quest to write the perfect narrative. She didn't have a fun bone in her pruny body.

With a heavy sigh, I tugged out my notebook and started jotting down whatever Mrs. Kendel was talking about. I couldn't wait to talk to Derek and see if his matchmaking had gone as well as mine.

Chapter 3

"Your mosaic is awesome," I whispered to Derek, who was sitting beside me in art class at the end of the school day.

He gave me a huge smile, putting down a tiny scrap of red paper he was about to glue onto his artwork. It was an image of a football player about to catch a ball. I wasn't a big sports person or anything, but his mosaic was good enough to draw even me in.

"I'd kiss you in thanks," Derek replied, "but I heard the teachers are cracking down on that."

I chuckled, putting down my scissors and trying to ignore the tingly feeling spreading across my lips at the thought of kissing Derek again. The last bell of the day couldn't ring fast enough for me.

"Tell me about it. That incident was in my class!" I dropped my voice even lower. "I'd paired up the two makeout bandits last night."

"You did good work," he said, admiration in his voice. "I heard it was quite a scene. Wish I could have been there."

Our art teacher, Mr. Bunch, who was leaning back in the chair at his desk, shot us a dirty look for talking when we should have been focusing on perfecting our craft. I tried to return my attention to my own crapola mosaic. It was supposed to be a woman playing a violin but instead looked like Picasso had vomited on my paper.

Oh, well. I had to accept there were some things in life I just wasn't good at. And art was apparently one of them.

Derek continued gluing the little squares of paper on his masterpiece, concentrating with the seriousness of a professional artist on his work.

As I glanced at the mosaic, a heavy lump of jealousy settled squarely in my chest. It was a good thing Derek was so cute and sweet because it would be easy to feel threatened by him and his multitude of talents. Everything he touched turned out perfectly.

Finally the gods of school took mercy on me and rang the last bell of the day. I cleaned up my art station and waited for Derek to be done so we could go to the library, where we'd be able to talk in privacy.

As he walked toward me, a bright smile on his face, I couldn't help the feeling of pride. He was looking at *me*, his girlfriend!

But is it magic induced, or real? a cruel little voice in my head taunted.

Shut up, I ordered myself.

But I couldn't help looking at the sparkle in his green eyes a little differently, with a little less pleasure than I'd had before. After all, hadn't I seen that exact same look on the guys I'd paired Maya up with? And on Andy's former boyfriend Tyler, when he'd been under the love spell too?

And on Mike this morning in English class, the moment he'd laid eyes on his love match Adele?

Derek linked his fingers with mine and gave me a warm kiss. We paced down the hallway, my gaze focused on the ground. I stared at my feet as we walked, unsure of what to say. Was I being paranoid, or was there a grain of truth in my worry?

Once in the library, we headed to our table in the back. Derek flung his backpack onto the desk and dug out his cupid manual, his PDA, and a notepad, putting them on the tabletop. He dropped into the seat across from me and shot me a devilish grin.

My heart thudded painfully in my chest in spite of my sudden mood change. God, he was so. Hot. I tried to shake off my funky mood and focus on the task at hand, taking out my PDA so we could get down to business.

"How many matches did you make last night?" I asked him.

He raised one eyebrow at me. "How many did *you* make?"

"I'll tell if you tell," I joked.

"I made eight," he admitted, shrugging his broad shoulders. "I was going to make more, but I wanted to pace myself."

"I made ten," I said with a smirk.

His other eyebrow shot up. "Ten? Sounds like someone's trying to up me."

"Hey, we never designated a set amount," I pointed out, crossing my arms in mock irritation. "So I didn't know I was upping you."

"How many people are still on your list to be paired up?" he asked.

I opened the document and scrolled down numbered names. Wow, I still had so many people to go. How would I get through them all before prom?

"I have almost a hundred and fifty," I stated, "excluding the ten matches I made last night."

Derek scratched his chin, deep in thought. "If we each average eleven good, quality matches a day, we should be able to get through our lists in two weeks . . . which is more than enough time to mend all those broken hearts before prom for the juniors and seniors."

Eleven matches a day. I could totally do that. And how sweet of Derek not to rub in that it was my fault there were so many broken hearts in the first place.

Could I ever live that down?

I thrust out a hand to him across the table. "You're on," I said with more bravado than I felt, shooting him a teasing smirk. "But you're gonna need to bring your A-game. I've had over a month on you as a cupid, you know."

Derek's mouth opened slightly in surprise from my assertive words, but then he clamped it shut and grabbed my hand, shaking it enthusiastically. "How about a little challenge to sweeten the deal, then?"

I swallowed. Who knew Derek was so competitive? It was a little intimidating, going up against the guy who was perfect at everything. But no way was I gonna walk away from a competition.

"What's the challenge?" I asked.

He stopped shaking my hand and turned my palm over to run his fingers across the tips of mine. I shuddered from the delicious swirls he painted on my skin. He had to know what he was doing to me, making it hard to focus!

"Let's see who has the most couples still together at prom time,"

Derek suggested. "The loser takes the winner out on a victory dinner wherever he—or she—wants to go."

A little healthy bet between the two of us wouldn't hurt anything, right?

"I hope you don't mind losing," I bluffed. "Because I'm totally going to order lobster for my meal."

Derek smirked. "We'll see about that."

Mallory Robinson: the two most evil words in the whole world.

I should have put a 666 beside her name because she was certainly the bane of my very existence.

I belatedly wished Derek would have put her on his list and matched her up without ever telling me because I didn't want anything to do with her.

That evening, up in my bedroom, I shifted in my computer chair and sighed, staring woefully at Mallory's name on my LoveLine 3000. Our friendship had dissolved freshman year because she'd thought I was crushing on her then-boyfriend James (who, by the way, has since been one of the most surprisingly successful cupid matches I've made—and not with Mallory, of course). And since that fight, things had only gone downhill.

How was I going to make a quality match for her? I was *so* not subjective when it came to Little Miss Prissy Pants.

Maybe I could work on someone else instead. Mallory was near the bottom of the list, so I'd start at the top and work my way down.

I cracked open the profile of the girl on the top of my list to see what I'd written from my observations of her in the hallways at school:

Name: Marie Sherry

Age: 14

Interests: Manga, anime, drawing. Seems to crush on every guy she sees (always stares at boys in the hall). Nose stuck in a book. Likes Hello Kitty (all over backpack and notebooks).

Style: Shy Loner

Ah, now I remembered her. Marie's the tiny freshman who always wears anime-covered stuff. She'd perch all by herself at a table in the corner of the cafeteria, scribbling in her notebook and chewing on her huge Hello Kitty pencil.

For a few minutes I scoured my profiles to find a suitable match for her and landed on a person who seemed perfect:

Name: Alec Marshall

Age: 14

Interests: Likes film critique and appreciation, and foreign/ indie music. Likes to bust out a beret sometimes. Possibly into guyliner.

Style: Quiet Nerd

Perfect—could two people be more suited for each other? Both were into the arts and foreign TV, so surely Alec would be able to hold lengthy conversations with Marie about the marvels of Japan. And they were both quiet people, so one wouldn't bug the other with constant conversation.

I composed a blank e-mail, adding Alec's and Marie's addresses in, and sent it. One high-quality match from my nightly quota down, ten more to go. I was already kicking ass and taking names.

But first an Internet break—time to connect to the mother ship.

I booted up my PC and deleted the insane amount of spam e-mail I'd gotten, then checked out Andy's latest locked blog entry for Maya's and my eyes only. In it, Andy dished about her date earlier this evening with Bobby Blowhard—er, Loward. I guess since they're dating now, I shouldn't call him by his nickname.

Bobby took me out to Hoggy's. You guys know how much I love that place—how sweet is he? Their corn chowder is KILLER good!

Anyway, while we were eating, we saw a guy propose to a girl.

I was stunned! I'd never seen a proposal before. Besides, it's not like we were at a fancy restaurant. But I figured maybe that was "their place" or something special for them.

I guess not, though. The girl blinked rapidly and said no, she just couldn't do it. Then she grabbed her purse and ran out of the restaurant, crying.

The whole place got really quiet and just watched the dumped guy in awkward silence. After a minute of sitting quietly in his seat, he dropped a wad of cash on the table and left.

I felt so, so bad for him. It reminded me how awful it is when you love someone who doesn't love you (aHEM, remember Tyler, anyone?). Thank God I'm not in that situation anymore, right?

Well, that was my night out. Hah—beat THAT, Fel and Maya!

I shook my head, baffled. How in the world do you get over the shock of a public humiliation like that? I guess you just pick up and move on . . . poor Andy did, after Tyler (the guy I'd originally matched her with) dumped her via a lame-ass note in the middle of the hallway. And look at her now, happier and more relaxed than I'd seen her in ages.

I left a quick comment, saying I was glad she'd had fun and that I certainly couldn't top her night, then shut off my PC, feeling strangely deflated. Hearing stories like that about heartbreak not only made me feel bad for the people involved but also reminded me of my own precarious situation with Derek.

Tomorrow night was my weekly TGIF sleepover with Andy and Maya. Maybe some chat time with my BFFs would help take my mind off the situation.

° ° °

"Omigod, I have to crank this song!" Andy hollered on Friday night, bouncing off my bed and running over to my iPod speakers. She turned up the volume, and the thumping bass filled my bedroom.

Good thing my parents were out to dinner, or else the House Nazi would surely be thumping *her* way up to my room to ground me. She was really picky about how loud the noise in my room could be.

Maya, who had been lying silently across my bed for a good half hour, stood and stretched. "I'm gonna go raid the fridge for snacks," she said. "I'll be back with supplies in a few minutes."

I nodded, then stretched out on my plush rug, trying to snap out of my funk. I was desperate to spill my guts to Andy and Maya about my worries, but how could I get it across without revealing the cupid stuff, too? It seemed impossible.

And so I kept my mouth shut.

But perceptive Andy seemed to pick up on my worries, anyway. She sat down beside me, crossing her long legs as gracefully as a ballerina.

"Okay, what's wrong, Felicity?" she asked me point blank. "You finally got the guy of your dreams. The school year's almost over.

You're gonna be a knockout in your prom dress. You should be doing the happy dance in your undies right now, not moping around like the world ends tomorrow."

I shrugged, staring at my ceiling. "You're right." I chewed on my lower lip. "But I can't help—" I stopped myself.

"Help what?" she asked, craning her head to look down at me. Her eyes were filled with worry. "Is something wrong?" She paused, and her voice took on a low, but teasing tone. "Derek didn't pop the question to you in Hoggy's and then you turned him down, right? I mean, what could be as bad as that?"

Knowing that Derek and I were only together because of a spell seemed like a pretty good one to add to the list of "crappy things that happen to couples."

I shrugged.

She leaned back against the foot of my bed. "He's absolutely crazy about you, you know. I've seen the way he looks at you, like you're his world. He seeks you out when you're not around. He talks about you to everyone. Derek is so in love, honey. So don't doubt your relationship."

I sat up, blinking rapidly. I shouldn't have been surprised that she'd pick up on what was bugging me; Andy was always intuitive about problems. But while I wanted to take comfort in her words, I knew the truth.

Maya swung my bedroom door open, bearing a large carton of ice cream and three spoons. She plopped down beside us on the floor and put the ice cream container in the middle, handing out spoons.

"I'm serious," Andy said to me, wagging the tip of the spoon in my direction. "You'll drive yourself crazy and analyze the life out of your relationship. Trust me. Just relax and let it be."

I took my spoon and dug into the vanilla bean ice cream, relishing the creamy taste. At least something always stayed constant for me, and that was ice cream.

"Don't you agree?" Andy asked Maya, who had been staring aimlessly to the side of the room.

Surprised, she jerked her head over to look at Andy, then shrugged wanly. "Yeah, I guess."

Wow, surprisingly nonwarm words. Maya was usually the first one to offer comfort to someone in need.

"I'm kinda tired," she continued, standing up and resting her spoon on the ice-cream carton's lid. She glanced at her watch, then turned the music down. "I think I'm gonna go to sleep."

Andy's brows scrunched, but she didn't say anything.

"Sure, do whatever you want," I said, trying to push down my reaction to Maya's apathy. But the stinging disappointment made it hard for me to keep my tone normal. "Make yourself comfortable."

Was she having problems? Or was discussing *my* love life just a little too boring for Maya?

Chapter 4

You know, if I thought *my* relationship issues were crazy, it was nothing compared to my brother Rob's. His flavor-of-the-week date for Sunday dinner somehow managed to surpass any other he'd brought home. And *not* in a good way.

When I opened the front door to let in Rob and his date, who was digging into her purse, she didn't instantly set off my radar—I couldn't see through any of her clothes, and all of her body parts looked real.

And then she lifted her face and made eye contact with me.

I blinked, stunned speechless.

Holy crap, she had to be several years older than my parents, not to mention at least a couple of decades on Rob, who was only twenty-one. She was almost old enough to be our grandma, actually. His date was still quite attractive, with a head of glossy, platinum-blond hair, but I could see gray roots where she was in need of a touch-up. The lines around her eyes and mouth were deep set, and she shot me a wide-mouthed smile.

"Well, hello," she said in a deep, throaty voice, patting me on the head. "You must be Felicity. You're just adorable."

Oh my God, she even talked and acted like a grandma. Seriously, did Rob have some kind of oedipal issue going on here?

Mom was going to Freak. The crap. Out. I almost couldn't wait to see it, if I wasn't so horrified myself.

Speak of the devil, Mom darted past me to the door to greet Rob and his date. When Mom saw his date, she froze in place, her face a stiff mask of shock.

"Guys, this is Mary," Rob said, smiling like nothing in the world was wrong. "Mary, this is my mom, Becky."

Wait. I'd heard of women like this before, on a talk show I'd watched when I was home sick. They're called cougars, known for prowling around bars for much-younger men to seduce. What in the world had made her pick my brother up, of all people?

Actually, an even better question was, what made him pick

her up? Did Grandma not show him enough love or give him enough Hot Wheels when he was growing up?

A surge of giggles bubbled in the back of my throat, and I forced myself to swallow it back down. Laughing was sooo not the appropriate response right now.

Mary took off her light jacket, revealing a purple dress shirt and black pants, and handed the coat to Rob. She cleared her throat, a raspy, grating sound that instantly pegged her as a pack-a-day smoker. Extra nice. "Hello, Becky," she said to Mom, thrusting out her hand. "Pleased to meet you."

"Welcome . . . Mary," Mom said, and moved aside to let them in, clearly trying to be as warm as she could. Her voice sounded like a frozen frog trying to talk. "You two can go . . . sit on the couch. Dinner will be ready shortly—we're finishing it up right now."

Mary gave a tight-lipped smile in response.

My mom went into the kitchen, and I followed Rob and Mary into the living room. They took a seat on the couch, and I sat on the recliner beside them.

"So," I asked Mary politely, "what do you do?" Other than hunt for younger guys to date, I meant.

She glanced at me for the briefest of moments, then looked

away, turning her attention to Rob like I hadn't spoken at all. "Sweetie," she purred, batting her lashes and running an arm down Rob's forearm, "I'm really thirsty. Can you get me a drink, please?"

Rob jumped up at Mary's words. "Sure," he said eagerly, then headed to the kitchen.

I leaned back in my chair and rolled my eyes. Great. This was going to be yet another superfun evening. And now I was left alone with the stuck-up Grandma Mary, who was spending her time glancing in disdain around the living room.

"God, this couch is so uncomfortable," I heard her mumble, shifting on the cushion.

My jaw dropped. "Excuse me—"

Mom's call for dinner interrupted me midsentence. Probably for the best, as I was about to say something rather biyotchy.

I followed Mary as she rose and went into the dining room, almost running into my mom, who was carrying a large baking dish of lasagna. Mary reached out a hand to steady herself on my mom's arm.

"Oh, dear," she said, eyes wide, and reached out for the lasagna dish. "Here, let me take that for you, Becky."

My mom's face twitched wildly. She looked confused about whether or not she should accept help from Rob's cougar date.

"Thanks," Mom finally said, handing the dish over. "That'd be great."

My dad came in from the kitchen, bearing a full tray of bread. He glanced at Rob's date, then looked away just as quickly. I bet Mom had already warned him about her, given the way he didn't freak out.

Dad took his place at the head of the table and passed the platter of lasagna around to Mary, who was on his left. "Hi. I'm Stephen, by the way," he said awkwardly.

"Helloooo," Mary said slowly, her eyes raking Dad up and down. She took the platter from him and sniffed it, smiling. "Oh, this lasagna smells just fantastic, Stephen. Did you make it yourself?"

The compliment seemed to relax him a bit. He smiled. "I did, thanks. It's an old family recipe passed down on my mother's side for generations. The bottom layer has sausage we buy fresh from a farmer's market. It gives it just the right kick."

Mary scooped an extra-large helping, then passed the tray over to Rob, not taking her eyes off my father. "Well, I can't wait to feast upon it," she said to him, her red-lipsticked mouth exaggerating her words as she blatantly flirted with my dad.

Dad flushed at her words and looked down at his food.

Ewwww! My jaw dropped, and I stared in horror. Grandma

Cougar was unbelievable. What a pair of brass balls this lady had. Yeah, my dad wasn't a bad-looking guy, but she was sitting right beside my brother . . . her date!

Mom, who was on Dad's right, cleared her throat loudly. "Let's eat," she said through pressed lips.

Awkward silence continued on and off throughout dinner, interrupted by requests to hand down salad or rolls or salt.

Mary wolfed down her first helping of lasagna, then went back for seconds, making sure to lick her fork clean after each bite. It was like she'd forgotten Rob existed and was focusing solely on making sure my dad knew she was into him—batting her eyelashes, laughing at all his jokes, the works.

Mom's cheeks burned with anger the entire time, but she was too polite to make a scene in front of everyone. Especially since Rob seemed oblivious to how crazy-talk whacko his date was. He continued to chomp away on his serving of lasagna.

Then Grandma Cougar's hand dropped into her lap, and she slid her gaze toward Dad. A moment later Dad flinched, then jumped up, shooting Mary an angry look.

"Excuse me," he said, dropping his napkin onto his plate. "I need to use the restroom." He left the dining room quickly.

The cow! I bet she'd tried to feel my dad's knee or something. Please, let it have only been his knee. Gross, gross, *gross*!

It was time for her to go, now.

"That was so tasty, Mom," I said, pushing my half-eaten plate of lasagna away from me. Normally I wouldn't have left any on the plate, since it was one of my favorite meals, but I could tell we were all ready to end this disaster of a dinner. And I was willing to do my part to help the cause.

Mom, who had spent the entire meal glaring at Mary and chewing her lower lip raw, grabbed my plate as soon as I moved my hands away from it. "Thanks, Felicity. Well, I hope dinner was enjoyable for everyone else, too."

Mary seemed to realize her welcome was long worn out. She glanced at her watch, sighing. "Rob, can we go now? I have somewhere to be shortly, and I'm dying for a smoke."

I saw my mom swallow back whatever words were on the tip of her tongue. Instead, she gathered up a few more dirty plates and headed into the kitchen. "Rob, Felicity, help me clear the table," she called out over her shoulder.

I gathered up the rest of the plates, while Rob snagged the cups. We made our way into the kitchen.

As I scraped off the excess food and loaded the plates into the dishwasher, Mom clutched Rob's upper arm in a death grip.

"Let me tell you something," she said quietly, but I heard the fire simmering in her voice. "If you ever bring another date like that into my home again, I will disown you."

I could tell she wanted to talk more about how flirtatious Grandma Cougar had been with Dad, but she also didn't want to hurt Rob's feelings. So she left it at that.

Rob chuckled, trying to wiggle out of Mom's grasp. "Okay."

Mom, obviously realizing Rob wasn't taking her seriously yet again, busted out The Evil Eye—the one look my brother and I had seen throughout our lives that had scared the living pee out of us. Our mother had a way of squinting her eyes in a wrathful, angry look that made you want to run upstairs and pray for divine intervention so she wouldn't beat the living crap out of you.

When Rob saw The Eye, he paused. "You're . . . serious."

"As a heart attack."

He swallowed, then nodded. "I'll try to find someone better," he said. "It's just hard finding nice girls."

She leaned in closer, still pinning him in her gaze. "Try. Harder."

My cupid radar went off, in a sudden brilliant plan. I closed the dishwasher and started the cycle.

It was time to help my brother find love. He'd been a student at my school recently, so couldn't I stretch the rules to make him count? Okay, he'd graduated four years ago, but still.

Finding Rob the perfect girlfriend wasn't going to be easy. In fact, it was going to suck a lot. Because Rob was a total weenie, and ever since he became a cop, he'd gotten even harder to deal with.

But I was a cupid, and it was my job to make love happen. I would make it a priority to follow him around and learn all I could about him to make his profile as accurate as possible. Surely there was someone out there who would both love my brother *and* not drive our family insane.

Mom hugged Rob. "Okay, go take her home. Please, for the love of God."

"Hey, Rob," I interjected as casually as I could, "how's your upcoming week looking?"

He looked at me suspiciously, and with good reason. I didn't normally ask him questions like that. "Why?"

Crap. *Think fast, brain!* "Um . . . because . . . I'm interested in . . . learning more about cops. I was hoping I could follow you and maybe see what you do." Wow, that was a killer save. Go, me!

"I think that's a great idea, honey!" Mom said, beaming. "Rob, set something up so your sister can shadow you at work, okay?"

He shrugged. "I'll e-mail you with my work schedule later. You can tell me when you want to come by the station."

Awesome! Once I had his schedule, I'd be able to pick the optimal time to spy on him. Plus, if I needed to ask anyone at his work questions, I could use meeting him there as an excuse. It was the perfect plan.

"Okay, thanks!" I said to him.

He and Mary left, with her surprisingly quiet. Maybe, somewhere inside, she realized she'd pushed it tonight. Probably not, though. Most people like that never think they do anything wrong.

But Mary would bother us no more. Because next Sunday Rob would be bringing a new date to dinner—a girl I'd picked out for him myself.

Monday morning at school I slipped behind my desk in English class right before the bell rang. I'd waited with Andy out in front of school for Maya as long as I could, but she hadn't shown up. She'd acted really bizarrely at my sleepover, and I was not only hurt by her distance but also worried that something was wrong. I'd even e-mailed her about it last night but never got a reply.

Mrs. Kendel shut the door to start class, then plodded over to her desk to pick up a big stack of papers. Gee, that looked promising. Not.

"Take out your notebooks," she ordered as she passed the packets down the aisles. "I want you to read the short narratives I'm handing out."

A few students grumbled under their breaths.

She stopped to glare at them, then continued, "Here's a list of things you need to identify when reading a narrative. Number one, who is our speaker? Number two, what is the tone of the story? Number three, what is the setting? And number four, what is the purpose of the story?" She glanced at her watch. "Okay, begin now."

I groaned inwardly, trying to focus whatever Monday-morning attention I could muster on the first narrative. Unfortunately, it was the most awful, dull story ever. Of course we couldn't get a story that would keep our interest.

No, the narrator of this enchanting piece of work was some older guy reminiscing about how he didn't get the dog he desperately wanted when he was a kid. Then his younger brother made him a pet rock that looked like a dog . . . but, of course, the narrator didn't want it because it wasn't a *real* dog, and he threw the rock out a window in a fit of anger. Eventually, though, the narrator came to appreciate that precious pet rock, as well as his family.

And now he keeps the pet rock on his desk.

What a *heart*warming story of love amongst brothers—I was moved beyond words. Okay, seriously, who wrote this crap? And even more important, why in the world would anyone publish it?

I picked up my pencil and started to write my less-than-flattering viewpoint of the story, when Maya came into the classroom.

Instantly I noticed her red-rimmed eyes and pale face as she scuffled over to Mrs. Kendel's desk. The teacher saw Maya's face also, and though Mrs. Kendel didn't comment on it, she had a worried look.

I heard Mrs. Kendel whisper the assignment to Maya, who nodded slowly in response, then made her way to her desk beside me.

"Hey, are you okay?" I whispered to her, having decided this was worth facing Mrs. Kendel's wrath.

Maya sighed and shook her head. She ripped a piece of paper out of her notebook and began writing furiously on it.

After a minute she folded it up and slid it over to me.

I clutched the note and shot a look around the room. Mrs. Kendel was flipping through some huge-ass novel on her desk. The coast clear, I furtively opened Maya's note and read it:

Sorry about our sleepover. I feel really bad. I know I wasn't acting like myself.

Things suck at home, and I just can't take it anymore. My parents told me yesterday that my dad's moving out and they're getting divorced.

I had a bad feeling on Friday that it was coming. :-(

I've been out of it all weekend.

I pressed a hand to my mouth in shock, blinking rapidly and rereading the paper. Maya's parents, splitting up?

No wonder she'd been so distracted on Friday. I'd be too, if I'd sensed that impending news like this was coming.

I wrote underneath her message:

I am so, so, soooo sorry. Let's talk more after class, okay?

We'll get through this, I promise.

After another glance at the front of the room to confirm I wasn't being watched, I gave the note back to Maya.

My stomach turned over itself in guilt. Maybe I hadn't been the best friend to Maya that I could have been because of my focus on work and Derek. But she needed me right now, and I was determined to help her in any way I could.

Chapter 5

The bell ending English class finally rang. I was desperate to talk to Maya about her parents' divorce. Plus, I didn't think I'd survive class if I had to read one more stupid narrative. Someone needed to have a serious heart-to-heart with Mrs. Kendel about her choice of reading matter, and soon.

"What's going on?" I asked Maya as soon as we exited the classroom door.

With a firm grip, I held her by the elbow and eased her to the side of the hallway, where we'd have a minute or two to talk.

Her eyes welled up, and she choked out in short bursts, "Dad . . . he decided he didn't . . . want to stay anymore. He moved out last night."

I hugged her tightly, wishing I could say the perfect words to take away her pain. "I'm sorry."

She sniffled against my shoulder. "And what's worse is that my mom still loves him. So this is breaking her heart—" She paused, drawing in a ragged breath. "Because I think she wants it to work out, you know?"

We pulled apart, silent for a moment. I had to say, I wasn't surprised her dad was the one leaving. I never saw him at their house—it was always her mom who was around. He, on the other hand, was always working. And I thought *my* dad was a workaholic.

"We'd better go to class," Maya mumbled. "We'll talk more at lunch, okay? If you talk to Andy before I do, you can fill her in. I'm sure she's wondering what's up."

"Okay. Hang in there."

After we separated, I got through my morning classes and finally made it to health, where I shared class with Andy. Unfortunately, I didn't get a chance to talk to her beforehand, so I tried to be patient and wait until lunch. In the meantime, when our teacher's back was turned to the class, I scrawled on a piece of paper:

Must talk after class. Private, please!

I slipped it to Andy. She opened it, then nodded in agreement.

Mrs. Cahill, our teacher, rambled on for the entire period about something or other. I think she was talking about making healthy food choices and cutting back on sugar intake . . . not that I was paying much attention to her. I pretended to studiously take notes while my mind was occupied with heavy thoughts.

There had to be something I could do to fix this divorce situation, or to help Maya take action somehow. I was a cupid— love was my business! I knew, however, that it would be pushing the limits of my cupid job too far to simply send a love e-mail to her folks. I wasn't supposed to matchmake anyone outside of school. I could kinda sorta justify matchmaking my brother, since he was a former student at Greenville High. But it was way too risky to attempt it with Maya's parents. If I got caught, surely I'd be canned.

Besides, when the e-mail's spell wore off in two weeks, there'd be no guarantee her parents' feelings would last. And that would just make the situation even worse.

Finally health class was over. Andy told her boyfriend, Bobby, she'd meet him at lunch in a few minutes. She and I headed to the cafeteria, during which time I filled her in on the situation.

Maya was already at the table with Scott, her boyfriend. He had his arm behind her, rubbing her back.

"Hey," Andy said in a soothing voice. She hugged Maya, then took the seat beside her. "You okay?"

Maya shrugged halfheartedly.

"This sucks," Scott said. He leaned over and kissed Maya's temple.

Out of nowhere a brilliant idea came straight from the heavens into my head. "Guys," I said, slipping into the seat on Scott's free side, "I think part of the problem is that Maya's dad and mom need a chance to reconnect."

"It's kind of hard to connect if you're not around each other," Maya said, bitterness creeping into her voice.

"But what if your mom was irresistible enough to make your dad want to be around her?" I said, warming to my idea.

After all, even though I couldn't risk sending love e-mails, that didn't mean Maya's mom couldn't do a cool makeover or something. And then Maya, Andy, and I could come up with some ideas to throw her mom in her dad's path. Surely, once he saw her looking her best, he would be drawn to her again.

Maya wiped a tear out of the corner of her eyes, looking over at me. "Maybe that could work. My mom does need a wardrobe update desperately. And this might be enough to help her feel happier, too."

"Well, I like it," Andy announced. "And I think we should do it." She saw Bobby entering the cafeteria and waved for him to come over.

I nodded enthusiastically at Maya. "Okay, let's take the rest of the day to think it over. We'll get together again and map out our plan. Operation Hook Up Mama Takahashi."

Maya gave a watery smile, sniffling again. "Thanks, guys. You're the best."

Andy squeezed Maya again. "Hey, that's what friends are for."

All through art class I couldn't stop staring at Derek's lips. We hadn't kissed all day—I swear, it should be illegal to go that long without it.

In between bouts of admiring my guy's mouth, I turned my attention back to my crappy mosaic. Maybe I should just scrap this one and start over, crafting the perfect image of Derek's mouth. Not that I'd do it justice or anything, but at least I'd have a vested interest in the project.

Derek must have read my mind. He glanced over at me, seeing my eyes on him again, and shot me a sly wink, puckering up and blowing me a couple of air kisses.

A hot flush swept over my cheeks. I could totally understand now why so many couples I'd matchmade couldn't stay apart from each other. Every moment we weren't together, he lingered in my mind. Because I'd had these feelings long before we'd started dating, I knew my love wasn't magic induced. But his could be.

Mr. Bunch stood in front of our tables, gesturing toward several large paintings in the back. "I need a student or two to carry these oil paintings for the art show to the teacher's lounge. Please be careful with them."

Derek and I looked at each other, then shot our hands up in the air.

The teacher nodded, heading over to his desk to write us a permission slip. "Okay, Derek and Felicity."

Yay! Time alone with Derek during class—what a rarity!

We gathered our slips and the artwork, promising not to dawdle in the hallway (yeah, *right*), and walked as slowly as we could toward the teacher's lounge. I tried to think of something intelligent and interesting to talk about.

Out of nowhere, Derek reached an arm over and pressed a warm palm against my stomach, stopping me in my tracks, then propped his paintings against the wall. He wrapped his arms around me and slid his lips over mine. I moaned softly and let my paintings lie against my leg, twining my fingers through his hair.

Oh, this was *so* much better than talking. We stole a few moments kissing, enjoying the sensation and heat, then regretfully stepped apart.

"Whew," I said, grinning wildly. My lips were puffy, and I knew my face had to be red all over from nervousness and excitement. I could have stood there and kissed him all day, if it weren't for the whole I'd-be-grounded-for-life-if-I-were-busted-by-a-teacher thing.

"That was great," he stated, his smile as big as mine. "I've been waiting all day to do that." He picked up his paintings again and brushed another quick kiss on my lips.

We walked in a warm silence to the teacher's lounge, where Derek opened the door for me. I stepped forward, then promptly stopped in the doorway, the air swooshing out of my lungs in a rush of surprise.

Mr. Wiley, my anthropology teacher, had Brenda, one of the

front office secretaries, pinned underneath him on the couch. Given their heavy making out, they obviously had gotten the love e-mails I'd sent them last night.

Derek, who couldn't see the scene, nudged me forward. "Hey, these paintings are getting heavy," he teased as he stood beside me, then sucked in a quick breath when he saw the scene in front of us.

At Derek's words Mr. Wiley jumped off the couch, his back stiff as a board. Brenda gasped and straightened her mussed clothes.

"Oh, Felicity," Mr. Wiley said, trying to affect an air of calm control. He pushed the knot of his necktie further up. "You surprised us. We were . . ." He paused, swallowing, and I could almost hear the gears in his brain cranking hard to come up with an excuse.

"You were . . . showing her how to do CPR?" I filled in helpfully, trying my hardest to bite back the laugh that threatened to come out.

Brenda nodded wildly, smoothing her hair. "That's right. Mack—I mean, Mr. Wiley was showing me the proper CPR technique." She paused, sliding her gaze over to him, and her lips parted. "He's really, really skilled at it."

"I happen to think you're a natural," he replied, inching closer to her.

Derek elbowed me in the side, confusion on his face.

"They were on my list," I whispered out of the corner of my mouth. To Mr. Wiley, I said, "Mr. Bunch asked us to drop off these paintings."

He nodded abstractly, his eyes back on his love match and hers on him.

Derek and I ditched the artwork and booked it out of there, closing the door behind us. We heard the door lock.

The laughter I'd been holding in bubbled out of me, and I cupped a hand over my mouth. "Oh my God, that was way too hilarious," I said. "They were all over each other . . . and during school hours!"

Derek shook his head, chuckling. He grabbed my hand, and we strolled back down the hallway toward art class. "You did a great job matching them up, Felicity."

"Thanks," I said, glowing from his praise. "They seemed like they'd be good together. I just paired them up yesterday."

"It always amazes me how hard the love spell hits some people. Mr. Wiley's always been a quiet teacher. He never struck me as someone who would be caught kissing someone, much less during school hours." Derek paused, mulling it over. "The love spell can change people from their natural impulses, can't it?"

The smile wiped off my face. How quickly I'd forgotten about the love spell cast on my own relationship. But Derek was right—look at how different people were when they were entranced.

I resisted the urge to look at him, forcing my voice to sound calm and even. "Why do you think that is? Is it because we have these impulses in us, and the spell brings it out?" Because that would be the optimal answer, and I was desperate to hear him agree with me.

Instead, he shrugged. "Who knows? Well, other than Janet."

"But the spell can't make you love someone who is absolutely wrong for you, right?" I pressed. "After all, that's why we have to do the compatibility charts."

"I don't know, actually. I haven't paired up people who are bad matches, so I can't answer that."

We got back to class, me feeling decidedly much less enthused than I did before.

"Everything go okay?" Mr. Bunch asked us.

I nodded, pushing down the bleakness that threatened to take over me. "Yup. Just fine."

Chapter 6

My Monday night meeting with Janet went well. She didn't mention the love spell she'd cast on Derek and me, so I didn't ask her about it. Besides, I felt uncomfortable whining to my boss about her doing her job, especially when sending love e-mails to two compatible people was the very same thing I'd done to my own friends.

I also didn't want to be a glutton for punishment. And obsessing over the genuine nature of Derek's love wasn't going to get me anywhere, not until I could figure out how I wanted to handle my worries.

So I decided to push the situation out of my mind and focus on one of the projects on my plate: finding a girlfriend for Rob. It was time to get that rolling.

As I drove out of Cupid's Hollow's headquarters that evening, I dug into my backpack and took out a notebook, where I'd plotted out my plan in great detail the previous night. It was sheer genius, and my only regret was that I couldn't share it with anyone else. I was tempted to run it by Derek, but I hadn't told him about matchmaking people outside of school, and I wasn't sure what his reaction would be. Maybe it was better to keep this to myself, then.

Rob was off work tonight, so I would spend an hour or so studying him and his behavior. This was the best way to complete his profile accurately, since I'd kind of lost track of his hobbies and habits now that he lived on his own. Then, per our agreement, I would go to the station and ask lots of questions of him and his co-workers, both to help round out my profile and possibly find any female colleagues who might be suitable for him.

After all, who better to be his potential girlfriend than a woman who understood the ins and outs of being a cop?

I pulled my car into a parking spot on the far end of the parking lot of The Dive, a bar I'd recently learned that my brother liked to visit (one of his former dates had blabbed on and on about how they met there—classy). When scheduling our meeting, Rob had told me he was going to meet some friends there.

He was probably going to pound down a few beers on the bar's massive back patio and then find his new flavor of the week.

Well, not if *I* could help it.

Hidden by the dark night shadows, I cast a furtive glance around me to make sure no one was coming, then grabbed my black long-sleeve shirt, to match my black dress pants, out of my backpack to throw over my shirt. I pulled my hair back into a ponytail and covered my head in a black baseball cap, then draped my binoculars over my neck, just in case I needed them for better observation.

There. Now no one would see me when I peeked through the fence slots of the bar's patio. It was the perfect way to spy on my brother in his natural element without actually sneaking into the bar and getting in megatrouble with the law.

When I noticed no one was around, I slipped my LoveLine 3000 into my pocket and got out of my car. Not that anyone would have heard me, anyway—the bass from the music on the patio thumped loudly enough to cover an elephant stomping through the parking lot.

Trying to look like it was absolutely normal for a seventeen-year-old girl to be hanging around outside of a bar, I maneuvered my way to a corner of the patio fence that was covered with bushes and waited for Rob to appear. As I hung out, I studied the patio, which was supposed to look like a tropical paradise.

Yeahhhh, the fake palm trees with neon-green paper fronds made the setting *so* authentic. There was also a giant tiki-themed counter near the door, where two female bartenders waited on customers.

Hey, wait . . . the one on the left, with the orange-colored tan and fried blond hair, seemed familiar. I think Rob had brought her over to the house for Sunday dinner a few weeks ago. I distinctly remembered this girl because she laughed like a hyena . . . which she was doing right now.

This totally confirmed my suspicions that Rob just dated any girl who happened to cross his path—he'd probably come here the night before dinner and, not having a date, asked the bartender if she was free on Sunday. Nice.

After a few minutes Rob and his work partner barreled through the bar's back doors onto the patio. They were laughing loudly and clapping people on the back as they made their way to the bar. Wow, my brother seemed to know, like, every person here. Party hard much, Rob?

I made a mental note to make sure whatever female I paired

him up with had other hobbies that Rob could be introduced to. He obviously needed to expand his horizons a bit more, and soon.

Rob didn't even have to order something to drink. The other bartender chick, some hoochie in the tiniest white T-shirt I'd ever seen, winked at my brother and said in a piercing voice that somehow managed to be even louder than the music, "Officer Rob, here's your beer, hon."

She slid a bottle down the bar's smooth wooden surface, and he caught it.

"Thanks, Maggie," he replied, giving her a smarmy grin. "Maybe I'll leave the handcuffs in the car tonight."

Ew, gag.

My brother and his attempts to flirt were vomit-tacular. I tried not to hurl as I peered through the fence slots, watching him make his way to a table. Crap, now I couldn't see him from my position.

With as much stealth as I could muster, I slowly made my way to my brother's table, using the fence as cover. He and his partner were alone, talking about the Cleveland Indians' latest baseball game.

I whipped out my handy-dandy LoveLine 3000 and began entering in my brother's profile:

Name: Rob Walker

Age: 21

Interests: Drinking/socializing. Sports. Cop equipment (including handcuffs, ick). Available women.

Style: Confident Player

Okay, obviously I needed more to add to his interests. I turned my attention back to Rob. Three women had joined him and his partner at the table in the few minutes it'd taken me to create his profile. I guess I shouldn't have been surprised.

"You're a cop?" the brunette asked Rob.

"Sure am."

She giggled, her overly red lips flying open as she breathed in deeply. "Hey, have you ever shot someone?"

Actually, that was a good question. I realized I didn't even know the answer.

Rob puffed his chest out. "Well, I drew my gun on a couple of thugs during a B and E last month." He paused, then leaned toward her in a conspiratorial manner. "That's 'breaking and entering,' in cop terms."

Unlike me, the woman seemed awed. "But did you actually *shoot* them?" she pressed him.

"Didn't need to. Just seeing my gun was enough to scare them straight."

I stifled a groan. Good grief, his ego was impossibly huge. He'd have to get over himself before I could find him the perfect—

"Excuse me," a deep voice said behind me, just as a hand clamped down on my shoulder. I was spun around, finding myself face-to-face with an on-duty cop. Crap!

"What are you doing, ma'am?" he continued, eyeing the binoculars dangling around my neck. He grabbed a flashlight out of his belt and flashed the beam directly in my face.

My heart thundered to about three hundred beats per minute. A flush stole over my face, bathed in the bright light.

This was bad. Really, really bad. I was in huuuuge trouble now, unless I could somehow charm him into letting me go.

"Oh, hello, Officer . . . ," I drawled, then smiled as confidently as I could, waiting for him to tell me his name.

"Banks," he said in a monotone, continuing to stare at me.

Okay, so maybe charm wasn't the way to go. Maybe connections would work better. After all, cops knew each other, right?

"My name's Felicity Walker," I said, consciously aware of the LoveLine 3000 currently hiding in my sweat-laden palm. It didn't seem like he'd noticed it yet, and I intended to keep it that way. "My brother's an officer in this city—Rob Walker. Do you know him? He's here in the bar, having some drinks. Off duty, of course," I hastened to add to the drivel I was spewing out.

The cop continued to stare at me expectantly, his face blank.

I kept rushing to talk, feeling the urge to unburden myself to this officer of the law. No wonder those people on the show *COPS* always blabbed on and on—the cops never spoke! "Well, anyway, I'm watching him. I'm . . . doing a report for class on police officers and trying to see if I want to be a policewoman myself. That's all."

Officer Banks's eyebrow rose. "Why are you watching your brother, dressed head to toe in black, without him knowing you're there?" He lifted his walkie-talkie off his belt. "Do you have a license or other form of identification?" he asked me.

"Uh, yeah." I opened my backpack, hands shaking, and carefully placed my LoveLine 3000 inside before taking out my license. "Here you go."

The officer studied the license. Then, over the walkie-talkie, he radioed in my identifying information.

A tense moment passed. I was thankful that at least the music was so loud, no one would notice what was going on on the back side of the fence . . . for example, my brother. If he knew, he'd rat me out to Mom for sure—and this was assuming I'd get out of this situation without needing to call her, anyway.

I prayed fervently in my head that Mom would remain blissfully unaware of whatever happened tonight. There would be a *serious* grounding or possible fatality in store for me. And with prom soooo close, I didn't want to do anything to incite her wrath.

Maybe spying on Rob hadn't been the best idea, after all. I could have found other ways to observe him instead of making myself look like a psycho stalker. I should take more time to thoroughly plan out my ideas from now on so I wouldn't get stuck in situations like this. No wonder things always went wonky for me.

The walkie-talkie clicked back on, and the person on the other end said some stuff to the officer, who then ended the conversation. Dropping the walkie-talkie back in his belt, he looked at me and handed back my license.

My heart thudded painfully in my chest, and all the air in my lungs froze in fear as I waited for him to tell me my fate.

"I'd highly recommend you get yourself home, Felicity. It's not safe for people to be out in the dark, and it looks suspicious.

And it's not a good idea for a minor to be hanging around establishments that serve alcohol." He gave me a meaningful look.

I exhaled through my nose, forcing myself to stay calm. "You're absolutely right, Officer," I said, my voice buoyant with relief. "That was dumb of me. I'll make sure to observe my brother in a much more public manner from now on." I was so happy to not be arrested or ratted out to my mom, I almost went to hug the officer in gratitude, but he didn't look overly friendly.

Slinging my backpack over my shoulder, I made my way to my car. Officer Banks followed me, probably to make sure I wouldn't try to continue lurking in the bushes.

I mentally slapped myself on the forehead. *Stupid idea, Felicity!* I'd never thought about the possibility of the bar being patrolled.

He watched me as I turned on my car and drove out of the bar's parking lot. I pulled on to the main street, careful to go slowly and use my turn signal—I didn't need to give him a reason to follow me—and headed home.

Step One of Operation Hook Up Mama Takahashi: get rid of all sweat suits. Unfortunately, it didn't seem like Mrs. Takahashi was taking too kindly to our suggestions.

She sighed heavily, crossing her arms over her chest. "I'm not sure I want to do this," she hedged, the crease between her brows deepening. "I know you're trying to do something nice for me, girls, but I feel comfortable in these clothes."

Andy, Maya, and I were standing beside Mrs. Takahashi in her bedroom after school the next day, ready to implement our plan to help her win back her husband. But I don't think any of us were prepared for Mrs. Takahashi's closet. How in the world could one person have accumulated so many pairs of gray sweatshirts and sweatpants?

"Mom, the first step in reinventing yourself is finding clothes that are comfortable *and* stylish. Please," Maya said, her eyes begging as she took her mom's hand, "let us help you. I promise, we won't make you wear anything that's itchy or awful."

Maya's mom gave her a weak smile. "Okay, I'm willing to give it a try. But no hot pink or other crazy neon colors."

We laughed. Andy took Mrs. Takahashi's other hand. "I think the first step here is to purge yourself of all these sweatpants."

I stepped forward and gathered them in my arms.

Maya cheered. "See how much room you have in your closet to add all those new clothes we're going to buy? We'll go ahead and take care of these sweat suits for you, okay?"

If by "take care of," she meant "burn," then I was totally game. "Before you know it," I said to Mrs. Takahashi, "you'll forget all about those sweat suits. I promise."

She smiled. I was glad to see she was going along with our plan. And now that the hard part was done, it was time for Step Two—taking her to the mall.

Chapter 7

All was going well with Mrs. Takahashi's superhottie makeover for the first hour or so. We found several outfits that flattered her figure. She even bought some honest-to-God makeup. Maya pulled me and Andy aside in the store Sephora and told us that her mom hadn't worn even so much as ChapStick in probably a dozen years.

Not that I was a makeup freak or anything, but wow. I couldn't imagine living with dry lips for that long.

Mrs. Takahashi walked out of Sephora, beaming as she bore two huge bags of clothes and makeup. Her face glowed from the skin-care samples the saleslady had put on her. She looked a good five years younger.

Maya followed closely behind her mom, bearing three more

bags. Andy and I, just behind, each carried other miscellaneous items that Mrs. Takahashi had purchased.

Andy suddenly sped up in her tracks and moved beside Maya's mom. "You need to go in there," she proclaimed, pointing to a store on her left.

Victoria's Secret.

Mrs. Takahashi shook her head, her cheeks flaming red. "No, really, I'm fine."

Maya blanched. "No. Way. Come on, guys, I'm sure she's already got plenty of . . ." She stalled on her words, trying to find a way to talk about her mom's underclothes in a public arena without freaking herself out.

Good luck with that. Having busted my parents midcopulation, I completely felt her pain. No teen wanted to think of her parents as sexual beings. Ick.

Andy handed me her bags, then grabbed Mrs. Takahashi's hand. "Trust me. You don't have to get anything trampy, I promise."

At her words, some older man, who was doing walking laps in the mall, slowed his pace and stared with interest at our conversation. Geez, guys were such perverts, no matter how old they were.

I shot him a glare, mentally shooing him away, then turned my attention back to Andy. "I don't think—"

"Aw, come on," Andy said, sighing with impatience. She tugged an uncertain, blushing Mrs. Takahashi across the mall's hallway toward Victoria's Secret. "Look, I'll take her inside, okay? You and Maya go grab an Orange Julius or something. Meet us in the food court in twenty minutes."

With that, they disappeared inside.

"I think I need something to drink," Maya said, looking like she was going to be sick. "I do *not* want to think about my mom buying teeny-tiny panties. I don't care if it *is* for Dad."

"Let's go to Orange Julius, then. And, hey, it's on me," I said, trying to be jovial.

Once there, we ordered a couple of fruit juices. I love their strawberry-banana drinks. So tasty.

To be honest, I was glad Andy was brave enough to take Mrs. Takahashi in Victoria's Secret. Great outfits didn't count for anything if you were wearing a grandma bra and big white bloomers underneath.

Maya and I grabbed a seat in the food court, waiting quietly for a minute for her mom and Andy to return.

"So, your mom got a lot of great stuff," I offered. "She's going to look fabulous. Your dad will hardly recognize her."

"Once she goes to her hair appointment tomorrow, she'll be a new woman," she agreed, tucking a strand of hair behind her ear. "She really needed to pamper herself. I'm glad you guys helped me talk her into it."

"No problem. Everyone deserves a chance to fight for the person they love," I said. "And maybe having an air of mysteriousness and newness around her will help draw him in."

Whoa, wait. My mind spun with a new possibility I hadn't considered. If reinventing herself would work for Mrs. Takahashi, why couldn't it work for *me*? I could reinvent myself, update my looks, learn how to be mysterious.

And Derek wouldn't be able to help wanting to be around me after the love spell ended next week because he'd be so intrigued by me.

Maya and I made small talk while we waited. In the back of my mind, though, I compiled a mental list of things I needed to do:

1. *New looks.* This required spending some of my hard-earned cupid money, but an investment in love is always a good thing.

2. *New attitude.* The best way to learn how to be alluring was to

study those who were good at it, like all the popular girls. In fact, I could also make sure to imitate their fashion sense, too, before going out and splurging on new clothes.

Andy, grinning from ear to ear, returned about half an hour later with a much more sober Mrs. Takahashi in tow. She was holding a V's Secret bag pinched tightly in one hand. Maya glanced at it in horror, probably hoping that the bag only contained a couple of pairs of full-coverage underwear rather than lots of tiny thongs.

"Okay, I'm ready to go home now, girls," Maya's mom said tiredly. "It's been a long day."

We left the mall and headed back to Maya's house, where Andy and I told the two of them good-bye, then walked home.

As soon as we rounded the corner, Andy busted up laughing. "Oh my God, I'm so glad Maya wasn't in there," she said, gasping for air. "You should have seen the underwear her mom picked out at first—it was the ugliest pair of granny panties ever. And they were, like, three sizes too big for her. Who knew Victoria's Secret even carried those?"

"Really?" I asked, giggling. "We should have known she'd go for those first."

"I swear, it took everything I had to convince her to try boy-cut panties. But once the saleslady got hold of her, Mrs. Takahashi had two new bras, and even a thong!"

"Yeah, I'm really glad Maya didn't witness that," I said, then gave Andy a hug when we reached my house. "Okay, I'll see you later!"

"Okey dokey!" Andy wandered off in the direction of her house.

I headed inside mine, still chuckling. No one was home, which was good. It gave me time to plan out how best to implement my latest and greatest idea.

I went right upstairs to my closet, flinging open the doors. First things first, it was time to get rid of the old so I could make room for the new, which I would be buying based on tomorrow's ultra-scientific study of the popular girls.

Good-bye, old Felicity! Hello, hotness!

The next morning at school I did what I never thought I'd do . . . I studied my archnemesis, Mallory.

As she talked with one of the senior football team members in the hallway before first period started, I took stock of her clothes so I'd know what to get when I went on my shopping spree tomorrow night: flats, tight jeans, and an Ed Hardy V-neck T-shirt covered in old-timey-looking tattoo pictures.

Then I noted her gestures and body language, making sure I was out of sight, of course—being busted for watching Mallory was *not* on the list of things I wanted to do today. She had her shoulder blades pressed against a locker, her back arched just enough to push her chest out and show off her cleavage.

Yeah, that one was going to get me nowhere, as I had none to show off. Oh, well. I'd just work with what I had, right?

Mallory nodded at something the jock said, licking her lips and tilting her head. "Really?" I heard her say. "God, you're so smart. I never knew that!"

He shrugged casually, leaning in toward her and pressing a palm against the locker right beside her head. "Not a lot of people do."

Oh, so she was stroking his ego, eh? *Good tactic, Mallory.* I grudgingly had to give her credit—her technique was clever when done with just the right amount of flirting, and Mallory seemed to intuitively know how to do it.

The bell rang, warning us to get to class. I headed into Mrs. Kendel's room. I noticed there was hushed whispering going on, and several people stopped talking when I got inside. Mrs. Kendel was nowhere to be seen.

What was going on?

Then I saw it. On top of my desk was a blood-red rose, a small note tied around the stem.

My heart pounded in my chest. Was that for me, or was it put on the wrong desk by accident? I was almost afraid to move closer in case it wasn't and I'd gotten my stupid hopes up for nothing.

"Go get it!" Maya whispered, waving me over. Her cheeks were flushed, and her eyes sparkled at me. "Oh my God, this is so cool! It was already here when we all got in the room."

I shuffled over, throat constricted, and plucked the flower off the desk. With a shaky hand, I flipped the note open and read the handwritten contents:

You're on my mind—all day, every day. Derek

I pressed the petals against my lips, sighing happily as I slid into my chair. I'd never gotten flowers before, ever.

Other girls were still staring in my direction. Even Adele and Mike unplugged their lips from each other long enough to shoot me a curious glance.

"Derek is sweet," Tessa, the girl behind me, said.

I nodded in agreement, still unable to speak.

Mrs. Kendel came into the room then, closing the door hard behind her. I dropped the flower onto my lap so she wouldn't see—I didn't want to get flack for introducing yet another romantic incident in class. "Okay, ladies and gents. Let's get to work."

As if I could concentrate. All period long I stroked the soft petals with the tips of my fingers. I don't think I heard two words she said. Nor did I really care. I just kept thinking, *Oh my God, he bought me a flower!*

When the bell rang, I darted out of the room, clutching the rose in my hand (I'd actually forgotten my books, so I had to run back in and get them), and waited in the hallway for Maya.

She popped out, then grabbed my upper arm and squealed. "Felicity! I can't believe Derek surprised you like this!" She sighed dramatically, pressing her hand over her chest. "This is so freaking romantic. You have to tell him he made my day."

I snorted. "You're telling me! I wasn't expecting this at all." After all, things like this didn't happen to me. They happened to Maya, or Andy, or other people who had been matchmade.

A sick thud hit my stomach. Derek had only given me the flower because he was under a love spell. I pushed the depressing thought aside just as quickly as it had hit me. Well, so what? Even if it was only spell induced, it was still a sweet gesture. And I wanted to focus on that, if just for a day.

"Okay, I gotta run," Maya said. "We'll talk at lunch." She beamed at me again, gave me a quick hug, then ran down the hall.

I made my way toward my second-period class, still holding the rose. I probably should have put it in my locker, but I didn't want to part with it, for fear that I'd hallucinated what was probably the most romantic gesture I'd ever gotten in my life.

Superpathetic? Yes. But I didn't care.

Mr. Shrupe's American history class was buzzing quietly, and the teacher was writing something on the board. When I stepped inside, a couple of girls pointed to my desk.

"Felicity, look!" Mandy said. "This was sitting here waiting for you."

No. Way. There was another rose, laid across my desk. Was this for real? I practically dove into my desk and whipped the note open:

If this rose could talk, it would tell you how special you are to me. Derek

"Please open your books to page two hundred and fifty-two," Mr. Shrupe said, oblivious as usual to anything going on in class.

I kept the roses on my desk this time, unable to stop looking at them all period. Two roses? This was insane. This was romantic.

This was unbelievable.

Every class period that day was the same. I came in, and some giddy person guided me to my desk, where there was a rose with a romantic note waiting for me. No one had seen Derek put the flowers on my desk. By lunch I had a good handful, which I of course carried with me to show a superexcited Maya and Andy.

I hustled through the rest of the periods, collecting roses along the way and eager to see Derek in art class. I was anxious to thank him for the incredible gift he'd given me today. Though I knew his gesture was clearly love-spell-induced, it was sheer magic for me to walk into each classroom and find a flower on my desk.

When I got into art, I settled into the seat beside him and put the big pile of roses on my desk, giving him a quick hug and kiss when the teacher wasn't looking.

"I missed seeing you today," he said, giving me that heart-breakingly adorable smile. "But I see you got my messages."

It equally thrilled and pained me, knowing his feelings for me, that beaming grin of his, these flowers, everything about our relationship was under false pretenses. My mood sank a little, but I forced myself to keep the smile on my face. After all, I already had a makeover plan in place to make things last after the spell wore off. It had to work.

"They are beautiful. Thank you so much. I'm sorry I missed you this morning." I glanced around, then whispered, "I had some cupid stuff to do." In a way, it was true—I'm a cupid, and I had some self-improvement to work on.

He nodded. "Gotcha. How go your matches?"

"Not bad," I replied. "I'm getting through my list every day and making fantastic progress." Before I could ask him how his were going, class started.

Mr. Bunch, who was fiddling with the projector in the back of the room, moved forward and dimmed the lights. "Today, instead of working on our art projects, we're going to watch a short film about one of my favorite artists, Jackson Pollock."

Oooh, a movie day! Another great surprise. It meant a chance to sit quietly beside Derek in the dark, where we could hold hands and spend a little bit of quality time together. Especially since I would have to leave right after school to run to the mall and get some new clothes and also interview my brother.

Sure enough, Derek slipped his warm, strong hand into mine. I squeezed it tightly and pretended to pay attention to the movie. But all I could think about was how to implement my makeover and knock his socks off.

I would prove to him I was worth this effort. It was time for Derek to see the new me!

Chapter 8

"And here's where we eat," Rob said to me later that afternoon as he led me into the little lunchroom in his police station, which consisted of a beat-up table and a microwave. "We'll do our interview in here."

I sat down across from him and whipped out my notebook, prepared with some questions to make our meeting look like an authentic interview. "Okay, what's a typical day like for you?" I asked him, pen hovering above paper and ready to write. "Where do you normally go?"

Rob leaned back in his chair, the front two chair feet rising off the ground. "Well, I like hanging out at The Burger Butler, but I also dig the lattes at Dunkin' Donuts." He paused, as if realizing I'd meant his job. "Um, that is, when I'm not out patrolling. I'm a beat cop, so I'm usually in my car pulling over drivers for moving-traffic violations."

I nodded intently, scrawling down that he liked coffee and burgers. Gee, how promising to know that life wasn't just about booze and chicks for him. It actually included other kinds of drink and flesh. "Okay, great. What do you think has been your greatest success as a police officer?"

After several seconds of silence, he said in a quiet tone, "Honestly? I don't think I've had one yet. I haven't really saved a life or jumped in the way of a bullet."

I froze, startled. It was rare for Rob to be serious.

"Maybe the things you think are small are actually big to someone else," I answered slowly. "Sometimes those little things mean a lot more to people. Remember that time at dinner when you told us you stopped a man from beating his wife again by throwing him in jail? I'm sure that meant the world to her."

He shrugged and leaned his front chair legs back on the floor, the badge on his chest glinting in the glaring fluorescent light overhead. "I guess you're right. But I'd like to experience those big moments sometime."

I chewed on my pen cap, then wrote *ambitious* and *awkward* on my list. It was good to see this side of him because it helped me understand that he could be vulnerable. Good traits for a guy.

For my last question, I'd asked him what was the worst thing he'd ever seen.

I swear, his eyes got a little watery when he described finding a near-dead homeless man in the alley a few months ago during a particularly nasty January storm. Fortunately, he and his partner had gotten the man to the hospital before hypothermia had caused irreversible damage.

When our time was up, I lingered in my chair, almost not wanting the moment to end. I couldn't remember a time when I'd felt this close to my brother. It made me feel good to be finding him a worthwhile girlfriend.

Speaking of . . . time to work on the next phase of Operation No More Hoochies in the Home.

"Rob," I said, "I think it would be great to talk to some female officers, if that's okay. I'd love to know what it's like to be a woman on the police force."

He nodded. "Sure. We have a couple of people in the station right now." He led me down the hall and through various rooms to get back toward the front of the station.

On my right I recognized Officer Banks, the cop who had busted me outside the bar.

Crap!

My heart rate sped up rapidly, and my palms began to sweat like a waterslide. Fortunately, Officer Banks hadn't seen me yet. I lifted my notebook and pretended to be fascinated by whatever I'd written in there as we walked by him.

It wasn't until after we'd turned the corner that I exhaled the lungful of air I didn't even know I was holding in. Another mini-crisis averted, thanks to my ninja–like reflexes.

We finally reached the front of the station, where several officers milled around, chatting. There was a bench where a few people sat waiting—one guy had a massive black eye, and the other was missing a few teeth. The officer standing close by was glaring at them both.

Whoops, guess fighting wasn't the right way to solve whatever problem you two had. I rolled my eyes and headed toward the two female cops, a brunette with a ponytail and a short-haired redhead, who were talking behind the desk.

"Heyyyy," my brother said, his bad-boy cop persona firmly back in place. "This is my sister, Felicity. She'd like to talk to you lay-dees about what it's like being a female cop. And I figured you two were the finest cops here, so you could answer her questions."

"For you, hon? Anything," the brunette said flirtatiously, winking.

"This is Officer Annette Lars," Rob said, pointing to the brunette. "And this is Officer Randi McPherson," he continued, indicating the redhead. "I'll be back in a few minutes to wrap up our interview." He took off.

Okay, two candidates for me to interview. Maybe luck would continue to be with me, and one of them would be the ideal match for Rob.

We found a few available seats in the corner of the room. I whipped out my notebook and wrote their names down.

"So, how do you get along with the men on the police force?" I asked them, hoping to discover how personable they were. "Have they ever had a problem dealing with you because you're women?"

Officer McPherson shrugged, smiling. "No issues. The men are usually respectful toward us, though you do have guys like your brother, who are a little flirty. But I've been here five years and never had a complaint against any of them."

"I agree," Officer Lars interjected. She leaned back in her seat, propping an ankle up on her thigh. "But it's sure nice having eye candy around, if you know what I mean."

She was *obviously* the saucy girl here, no bones about it. Whereas that might be bad for some people, it seemed like my brother responded to it with no problems whatsoever. I jotted that down underneath her name.

I cast a furtive glance to their hands. No wedding bands or engagement rings on either of the two candidates. Another good sign. However, that didn't mean they didn't have boyfriends . . . or husbands.

"How do your . . . families or significant others feel about you being an officer?" I asked, priding myself on the cleverness of the question.

Officer Lars grinned. "I don't have anyone at home except a cat, and she doesn't seem to be bothered by my job."

I chuckled. "Fair enough."

"Well, my boyfriend seems supportive of my job, though I'm sure he wouldn't like me being in harm's way," Officer McPherson said, giving me a knowing grin and a shrug.

Bingo. Looks like we just narrowed down the playing field. Time to home in and make sure Officer Lars would suit my brother.

After writing more notes in my journal, I asked, "What do you two like to do when you're not working? I'm sure it's good to relax after a busy day."

"My boyfriend and I go out to dinner, or I go shopping when I'm off," Officer McPherson said.

"I usually hang with my girlfriends," Officer Lars said. She tucked a loose strand of hair back into her ponytail. "We go out to dinner and a movie, or occasionally to a bar." She paused, then looked at me. "But I never, never drive drunk," she said. "We always have a designated driver. Having a cop busted for a DWI is very, very bad."

So she liked to party but was smart about it? Definitely a bonus.

Rob came back into the room and headed over to us. "You all done?" he asked. "These ladies probably need to get back to work."

They both beamed at him.

"It was a pleasure," Officer Lars said to him, her eyes sparkling.

"Is it okay if I get your e-mail addresses, in case I have further questions?" I asked them both.

They quickly scribbled their e-mails down on a clean piece of paper.

"Please feel free to talk to me anytime," Officer McPherson

said. "It's been a pleasure. I like seeing young girls take interest in typically male careers."

She was totally awesome. Even if she already had a boyfriend. I decided her guy was one lucky man.

"Thank you," I told her, shaking her hand. Then I shook Officer Lars's hand. "I'll be in touch," I promised her.

And I would. Because I was totally going to send love e-mails to her and my brother. Tonight.

Chapter 9

I should have realized the fake eyelashes would be a bad idea.

"You okay?" Derek asked me from across the table, his brows knit together.

We were on our official "second week together" date at Starbucks on Thursday night, where I was carefully sipping a delicious Green Tea Frappuccino through a straw to keep from wearing off too much of my brand-new pale pink lipstick.

As part of my makeover plan, I'd realized that most of the popular girls played up only one feature of their faces. So I'd decided on making my eyes pop even more than usual by gluing on some fake eyelashes I'd found in the drugstore. To balance it all out and keep from looking like a mini-hooker,

I also wore natural-toned makeup on my cheeks and lips.

"Yeah, I'm fine," I answered Derek, tossing my hair and giving what I hoped was a flirtatious smile. "Why?"

He squinted and leaned over, studying my face closer. "Your right eye seems . . . off. Do you have something in it? Need a napkin?" He held one toward me.

I waved it away and blinked rapidly for the four-thousandth time, casually slipping my finger along the edge of my eyelid to press the lash back on. In my head, I prayed to the makeup gods that it wouldn't fall off. It seemed I hadn't put enough glue on (nor had I been smart enough to bring that glue in my purse for emergencies), so I was in constant peril of ruining the date and embarrassing myself through the loss of my fake eyelashes. Lovely.

Well, no time to worry about that. I needed to get my flirt on. Good makeup was only going to get me so far, after all. Right now I needed to tease him, draw him in with my masterful allure.

"Oh, I'm just winking at you, you hottie," I answered him coyly. "You look so good today."

And he did. It was a good thing Derek was sitting across the table from me because he'd need to wear a rain jacket from all the drool I'd get on him. His broad shoulders were well defined in a jersey-style shirt. And I'd seen earlier that his butt looked better than usual in a pair of nicely fitted jeans.

Taaaaaasty. I was one lucky girl.

He took a bite of the superfudgy brownie he'd bought. "Thanks. So, how are your matches going? I'm almost through my list, with around twenty-five couples left to make. I should be done by the end of this weekend."

I swirled the straw for my drink between my index finger and thumb, then mimicked a trick I'd seen one of Mallory's friends do at lunch yesterday—she'd rubbed the end of the straw across her lower lip, then had taken a sexy little sip.

Except no drink was coming out.

I took a bigger sip through my straw, and a surge of icy cold, thick drink flooded my mouth and slid down my throat.

"My—matches—," I hacked out, trying to push away the impending brain freeze, "are fine—thanks."

Yeah, this was going well. How come I never saw Mallory lose an eyelash or get brain freeze?

"Might wanna take a bit smaller sips," Derek pointed out.

"Yeah, I kind of figured that out," I snapped, unable to keep the aggravated tone out of my voice.

"Just trying to help," he mumbled, looking down at his mug.

Crap. Okay, I wasn't supposed to alienate him or make him feel bad. This night was about giving him a good impression of me that would last past the spell wearing off.

I glanced at my chest, tugging down my V-neck shirt just a wee bit more. Not that it made me suddenly grow cleavage or anything, but the action seemed a little more in line with my makeover plan.

"I'm sorry, honey," I finally purred, leaning forward. I would have winked at him, had I not been afraid of my eyelashes flying off. Now that would have been a disaster I could never fix. "Brain freeze gets me every time. I should have listened to you, though, because you're sooooo smart."

I almost ralphed with how hard I was laying it on, but if I'd learned anything from watching Mallory, it was that flattery got you everywhere, especially with guys.

Derek shot me an odd look. "Um, okay. Anyway," he continued, pulling out his LoveLine 3000 from his back pocket, "I was thinking we could work on making this evening's matches. I haven't gotten to mine tonight, and it's fun getting your opinion on things."

I didn't want to work; I wanted to seduce! But maybe this would give me an unexpected opportunity. Grabbing my purse and drink, I slid out of my seat and over to the available space beside Derek.

Why didn't I think of this before? I could "accidentally" press up against him. Surely that would drive him wild!

I pulled out my LoveLine 3000 and turned it on, bringing up my list. "I still have . . . thirty couples to match up," I said, leaning toward him with an arched back.

He scrolled down through my names, paying absolutely no attention to my chest. "This looks great," he said, smiling at me. "You've got some good people still on here. I'm sure it'll be easy to pair them up."

Dude, what gives? Was I doing this wrong?

Then awareness struck me. I was forcing it too much on him. If I wanted to win his attention, I needed to draw *him* to *me*, not press him. I would be the spider with the pot of honey, sitting pretty in my parlor, luring in the unsuspecting fly. Or something like that.

After all, guys liked what they couldn't get, right?

I sucked my chest back in, drawing my LoveLine 3000 back toward me. "Yup, and I have a strategy in place to get these matches done fast and accurately."

I had no such thing, of course, and was bluffing through my phony eyelashes, but I needed to appear like I had some mysterious smarts that he didn't know about.

"Oh, really?" Derek asked, curiosity written on his face. He raised one eyebrow. "So what are you going to do?"

Crap. Maybe I should have thought this through better.

"Ummmmmm," I stalled, then finally said in what I hoped was a husky voice, "that's for me to know."

Yeah, not the most mysterious thing I could have said, but it worked. He stopped pressing me about the subject.

"So, I was thinking of pairing up Sam from the soccer team, but I wasn't sure if this girl would be right for him, or this one," Derek said as he leaned closer to me, pointing at some names on his list. "What do you think?"

Yarrrrr. I could smell the clean scent of his cologne, and it took all my willpower to maintain my new mysterious persona and not jump on top of him. I hadn't thought to wear perfume for our date, so I made a mental note to snake some of my mom's to wear to school tomorrow. Something told me that the baby powder lotion I usually wore wasn't quite as alluring as I wanted.

"Well, I happen to know that Ellen," I said, pointing to the first girl on his list, "is big-time into acting. She was the star of the senior play."

"And Sam was in it too. I forgot about that," Derek admitted, a slow grin spreading across his face. "Very clever, Felicity."

"Thanks. I've heard I have good ideas every once in a while," I joked, then stopped myself.

I was supposed to be mysterious, not my usual goofy self. *Concentrate!* My love was on the line, and no way was I going to lose him.

"And I've learned a thing or two while being a cupid," I added, hoping I sounded wise and all-knowing.

Derek's eyes connected with mine, and I stared back. It was an intense moment; all the background noise of the café faded away.

We leaned toward each other, our mouths mere inches apart. His eyes became dark, hooded, and I closed mine, mentally drawing him into my spidey parlor.

"Hey, man!" I heard a guy say.

My eyes flew open. A few of Derek's jock friends surrounded our table. Right behind them Mallory and two other girls who didn't go to our school were gathered in a small circle, staring boldly at me as they whispered under their breaths.

Of *course* they were here. When we were by ourselves, it was easy to forget that Derek was superpopular.

I turned back toward the table and steepled my fingers like I was deep in thought, using the gesture to cover up smoothing down my eyelashes in the inner corners. They were starting to peel off my eyelids again.

Okay, no way was I going to have one of my fake lashes fly off while Mallory was around. Time to ditch them. I would play around with how much glue to use later at home, but for now they were more of a liability than an asset.

"Dude, what's up?" Jay asked, thumping Derek hard on his back.

He stood to face them, deftly slipping his LoveLine 3000 into his back pocket before anyone could see. "Hey, man, not much. We're just having some coffee."

The girls squeezed into the booth seat across from us, plunking their drinks down on the table and sighing heavily.

"God, I'm so bored," one of the blond chicks whined to the other. She blew a huge pink bubble and let it pop. "Why are we here? I thought we were going to a movie."

"I don't want to see a movie," the other girl replied. She took a sip of her drink. "Everything in the theater is utter crap right now."

The guys kept talking, oblivious to what the girls were doing.

Taking advantage of the fact that none of them paid me any attention, I leaned over like I had to fix my shoelace. Then I slipped my compact mirror out of my purse. Under the table I ripped off my eyelashes and crammed them in my mirror, snapping it shut.

One problem solved. Now, how could I get rid of my other problem, currently sitting across from me?

"Ew, what's in that?" Mallory asked me, sneering at my drink. "It's *green*."

"It's a Green Tea Frappuccino," I explained, trying not to sound defensive. "They're actually really good."

"Oh. Well, I hate tea." She blanched. "Give me an espresso any day of the week."

Gee, color me surprised. My temples started to throb. I had to think fast. It was torture to sit here and let her and her stupid friends ruin my evening.

I turned toward Derek and tugged gently on his sleeve. "I'm sorry, honey," I said, grimacing, "but I have a bad headache."

He studied my face in concern. "Okay, let's get you out of here. Do you want to stop at the store on the way home and pick up some pain pills?"

I shook my head. "Nah, I have some in my cabinet."

We left, with me not paying one bit of attention to Mallory, her friends, and the jocks, who quickly took over our table and started yapping amongst themselves. Buh-bye!

I had to admit, it was wonderful being nurtured by Derek, who insisted once we'd reached my front porch that I needed to take some aspirin and go right upstairs.

"And call me if you need anything," he insisted, opening my front door for me. "I mean it."

"I will, I promise."

God, he was so sweet and thoughtful. I gave him a big bear hug. A sensation of fear tickled my chest over the panic of possibly losing him, and I tried to fight it down. Granted, I'd sucked big-time at my attempted seduction-slash-makeover, but I'd get another chance to try again tomorrow.

After all, I still had six whole days until the love spell wore off. More than enough time to make true love happen, right?

Chapter 10

Thank God it was Friday . . . and lunchtime! I was starving and ready to nosh on my sandwich.

All this acting-mysterious stuff was way harder work than I'd realized. If I'd actually liked and respected Mallory, I'd have to give her props for keeping the gig up all day, every day. How tiring to constantly perform, to keep up a persona.

Not to mention the high makeup maintenance. Good grief, I must have reapplied my lipstick about forty times so far today.

Dropping into the seat beside Maya, I pulled out my PB&J sandwich and started digging in.

"Oh man, I'm totally dying of hunger," I proclaimed between bites. Right then I didn't care about taking dainty nibbles.

Maya, who was eating a slice of pizza, giggled and shook her head at me. "I can see that."

"Most guys can appreciate a girl who's not afraid to throw down," her boyfriend, Scott, added.

"That must be why you like sitting at our table," I offered. "Because Maya and I know how to eat heartily."

Andy and Bobby, bearing lunch trays, showed up at our table and sat down.

"Oh my God, could you believe what Mrs. Cahill said in health class today?" Andy asked us all, picking up her pizza slice as she talked. "She totally—"

When her eyes hit me, Andy stopped midsentence.

I frowned under her scrutiny, squirming slightly in my seat. "What?"

Everyone else stopped eating and stared at me too.

Oh, goodie. Did I look like a total freak or something? Was there food on my face? Had my boobs fallen out of my low-cut shirt?

I sneaked a quick peek down at my chest—everything was still in place, thankfully. Then I patted a napkin on my cheeks and mouth to make sure there wasn't anything weird on there and ran my fingers along my eyelids as subtly as possible. Whew, the lashes were still glued on just fine.

Andy tilted her head, chewing on her lower lip. "Something's different about you. I can't figure it out—"

"Well, I got some clothes. And I'm playing around with different makeup styles," I interjected, not wanting to point out my fake eyelashes for obvious reasons. I was hoping I'd just look more appealing to everyone without people being fully aware of why.

After playing around with my lashes last night, I'd finally figured out the perfect amount of glue to use. Presto change-o, I was a newly made goddess. It did bother me a bit, though, that Derek hadn't said anything about my new appearance. But maybe he was waiting until we were alone to tell me if he liked it.

Or maybe he doesn't like it, the evil whisper inside my head said.

Shut up, I ordered myself. Wallowing in self-pity and fear wasn't going to keep Derek's love. "By the way, does my lipstick still look okay?" I asked Andy, trying to distract myself from my woes. "I'm trying out a new shade of pink."

"Yeah, your lips look fine," Andy said, raising one eyebrow at me but saying nothing else.

I sat in silence and picked at the rest of my lunch, my appetite soured because of my secret doubts and the less than warm reception I'd gotten from everyone so far from my makeover. Maya and Andy talked for several minutes about Ms. Chan, who had told her class today that she was going on sabbatical next year to live in India. Talk about out of the blue surprises . . . especially since we'd heard that a male freshman English teacher was going to do the exact same thing.

What a coincidence.

Something told me those two had been paired up with each other by Derek.

Lunch ended, and Andy and I headed to anthropology together.

"Okay, we're alone now," she said in a low voice as we paced through the hallway. "You have to tell me what's going on, because you look very different, and you're acting really weird."

The longing to open up to my best friend caused an avalanche of words to spill forth from my lips. "I'm worried that Derek may not really love me like I want him to love me so I was hoping if I dressed exotically and seemed interesting and different that he'd be drawn to me and wouldn't want to leave."

I stopped and sucked in a few deep breaths. Whew, it felt so good to unload that off my chest.

Andy grabbed my elbow and tugged me to the side of the hallway. "Okay, all of this makes sense now. I wondered why you were suddenly concerned with your makeup and clothes. And why your eyelashes suddenly looked thick and luxurious," she added in a dry voice, giving me a knowing look.

A flush crept up my neck and cheeks. "Yeah, well, it works for other girls around here," I mumbled. "They keep guys wrapped around their fingers."

Her face softened. "Look, I know Derek is an awesome guy and that you're crazy about him, but is he worth changing yourself like this?"

"To me, he's definitely worth fighting for," I said quietly. "I love him, and I need to keep him attracted to me."

The second bell rang, letting us know we were late for class.

"Let's go. But we're gonna finish this conversation later," Andy said as we started walking again. "Mr. Wiley's really uptight and hates when people are late."

I snickered, remembering the way he'd looked when I'd busted him making out with the school secretary Brenda in the teacher's lounge.

"Well, I'm willing to bet he won't yell at us," I casually replied, knowing I was about to drop some interesting info on Andy. "He's been . . . occupied the last few days with his own romance."

Her jaw dropped. "Wait, you know gossip that I don't? Oh, man, I cannot *wait* to hear all about this."

Okay, only thirty couples left to make. Just thirty, and then I'd be all done with my list. I could do this.

From my corner of the library, I saw two couples cuddling at nearby tables. One was a pair of seniors who must have been on Derek's list. I instantly recognized the Hello Kitty backpack beside the other girl—it was Marie, the freshman I'd matchmade with Alec. Finally, a chance to see how these two were doing! I hardly ever saw them around school.

"Oh my God, I can't wait to see that series," Marie was saying to him, clapping her hands in excitement. "It's huge in Japan. They should have brought it to the U.S. long before now." She dropped her voice. "I heard they're hiring American actors to do the voice-overs."

Alec shook his head, his face filled with disgust. "I know. It sucks that we get these horrible voice-overs for the series they release here. Because America is obviously too stupid to understand or appreciate original Japanese casts. But whatever. When I move to Japan, I'll see the originals for everything."

Marie sighed. "I desperately want to go to the Hello Kitty store in Japan. They have everything you could possibly want. I could die happy in that place."

"Hey, wanna go watch something at my house?" Alec asked. "I just got the newest season of *Bleach*."

"Yeah, that sounds great!" Marie stood and slipped her backpack on.

The two of them left.

I grinned. Watching them together, speaking their nerd language so happily with each other, made me feel pretty good. It was probably a good thing my friends weren't here with me. Andy would have seriously ripped on them had she overheard that conversation.

I whipped out my LoveLine 3000, wishing Derek were with me. His dad needed him to help out at the sports shop after school today, though, so I was going to chill out here in the reference section for a couple of hours until I met Andy and Maya for our TGIF sleepover. And the best way to be productive, since I'd already finished most of my homework, was to make more couples.

But for some reason I couldn't concentrate. An image of Andy's smiling face popped in my head. Boy, watching people fall in love always surprised me. I never would have expected her to hook up with Bobby, not in a million years. She was gorgeous and fun, and he was short and eccentric, to say the least. It was so weird that the two of them were somehow drawn together, all because of working on our health class project as a group.

Or . . . was that the real cause?

Letting the LoveLine 3000 rest in my lap, I mentally replayed last Wednesday, when I'd finally found out that Andy and Bobby were going out. I'd shown up at the cafeteria to find the two of them cuddling close. And later I'd realized they'd been talking to each other even when I wasn't around.

Was it possible that Derek had matchmade Andy and Bobby? After all, he'd become a cupid by then and obviously had his own quotas to make.

The idea drew out conflicting emotions in me. I was glad to see Derek was intuitively good as a cupid—he was pairing up couples who, upon first glance, might not look like they belonged together. And from the way Andy and Bobby shared jokes and hobbies, it seemed quite possible that they wouldn't break up even after their spell wore off.

But on the flip side of the coin, what did that mean about *me*, as a cupid? Because I was obviously missing something big by not seeing these potential couples.

I lifted my PDA and stared at the names on the list that I'd already matched up. My heart started to race as I scrutinized each name and the person I'd paired them up with. What couples had I messed up because I hadn't made their profiles detailed enough, or thought "outside the box" in my matchmaking?

Fear bubbled below the surface of my skin, and I looked again at the people I still had to match. Sixty individuals, waiting for me to find them the perfect love match. But could I do the job justice? What had once seemed like such a cakewalk now felt almost impossible.

As my thoughts entered a spin cycle, the couple near me that Derek had matched walked out of the library, fingers linked, leaving me alone.

Okay, let's not be ridiculous, I told myself. *Focus.* No sense freaking out right now. I could do this.

Besides, just because Derek was a good matchmaker didn't mean I was bad. We could both be good at our jobs. I'd made some high-quality couples that were still going strong, like James and

Mitzi, or DeShawn and Marisa. I mean, for all our teasing and bravado, it wasn't *really* a competition between me and him . . . right?

Well if it was, I was never one to back down from a challenge.

I picked the next guy on my list, a sports nut named Dale who I'd seen at most of our school's basketball games, then scrolled down to find the perfect match for him from the remaining people on the list. Hmmm, Deanna, a girl in my American history class, might be a good one, since she was a huge hockey fan.

I composed the e-mail, adding their two names, and went to hit send but then paused. Just because two people liked sports didn't mean they'd be a great couple. Did they have enough in common with each other to make them ideal matches? Or was there someone else who might be better for him?

A sudden sick feeling hit my stomach. I wasn't ready to send this e-mail yet. I needed to do more research to make sure these two were actually right for each other. Maybe I could enrich their profiles first.

My course of action decided, I turned off my LoveLine 3000 and tugged out my American history book and notebook to study for a test next week. Not that it was a faboo alternative, but at least there I knew what I was supposed to do.

"Guys, I need your help," Andy said to Maya and me at our TGIF sleepover. She wrung her hands and swallowed. "But you have to promise not to tell anyone. Because I am totally. Screwed. Unless I get this fixed."

Crossing my pajama-clad legs, I sat up on Andy's bed. "Well, color me intrigued."

Maya perked up too, pulling her attention away from the *Cosmo* she was reading. "Yeah, what's going on?"

Andy pressed her index finger against her lips and went over to her door. "Just follow me and be superquiet, please. My mom is in bed, and I don't want to wake her up."

Silent as the grave, Maya and I followed Andy down through her house and into the three-car garage. And yes, they actually had three cars to fit in there. Andy flipped on the light switch and led us to the covered car at the far end, tugging back the black cover.

The first thing I noticed was the smashed-up corner of Andy's dad's fire-red Porsche. The headlight was broken, and the hubcap was missing. Ouch, that was bad.

I exhaled loudly. "Whoa, what did you do?" I asked.

Maya grimaced, squatting down to check out the damage. "Yeah, that is so not good. How are you going to get it fixed?"

Andy dropped the tarp and sighed. "That's what I wanted your help with. My dad's on a business trip, so he hasn't seen it yet. But when he gets back, he's gonna want to drive it." She paused, tilting her head. "I think I hear something. Let's go back upstairs and finish talking."

We crept back up to Andy's bedroom and closed the door behind us, taking our spots on her bed again.

"Okay," Andy said. "This was really, really stupid of me, and I've learned my lesson. And I'll never do it again, I promise." She held up her fingers in the Boy Scout's–promise kind of way. "So earlier today I decided to treat Bobby to dinner. I wanted to do it in style, so I—" She stopped. "Well, I'm sure you can figure it out. Home alone, with the keys to the most awesome car ever." She grimaced, shaking her head. "I had no problems driving to pick him up or going to the restaurant, but after I dropped him off and was heading home, I got into a . . . minor accident."

Andy's parents were usually pretty chill, but if they found out what she'd done, they'd ground her forever. That car was her dad's baby, and everyone knew it.

"Oh, no!" Maya exclaimed. "Did the police come?"

She bit her lip. "Well . . . I didn't exactly report it. I was digging through my purse to find my cell phone and accidentally hit a mailbox. I was so freaked out, I panicked and just drove home. Then I threw the tarp on over the car and decided to see if you guys could help me figure out what to do."

Maya twiddled her feet off the edge of the bed. "What if you . . . told them the car had been temporarily stolen?"

"And then brought back into their garage? I don't think they'd buy that," I said.

We sat in silence for a moment, trying to think of the perfect solution.

Andy sucked in a quick breath. "There has to be something I can do. And I figured three heads were better than one." Tears welled up in her eyes, and she sniffled. "I'm afraid if I tell my dad what I did, he'll ground me from going to prom."

"We'll make everything better," I said, hugging her. "Don't cry."

Maya rubbed her chin. "I heard if you divert your attention to something else, the solution to problems will come from your unconscious mind when you least expect it." She glanced around the bedroom and snagged the *Cosmo* she'd been reading. "Okay, let's take a quiz to distract ourselves. I bet afterward we'll know what to do."

Andy shrugged halfheartedly. "I guess so."

"Okay." Maya thumbed through a few thousand pages of stinky perfume ads, then stopped. "Aha, here we go. *Are you made for each other? Take this quiz to find out.*"

I groaned. I didn't need something else to remind me of my woes with Derek. "Can we do another quiz, instead?"

Maya's eyes studied me with concern, but she nodded silently, then flipped through *Cosmo*. "How about . . . *What's Your Ideal Career?*"

Now, that was more like it. I couldn't wait to see what this quiz would reveal about me and my best buds.

Chapter 11

"A therapist? Really?" I asked. I didn't know why I was surprised, though—it's not like the quiz would have cupid listed as one of the choices or anything. But I guess I wasn't expecting to hear I'd be a good shrink.

Maya, who had tallied up my answers first, nodded, the corners of her mouth curving up. "I totally believe it. Everyone comes to you when they have problems. And you love helping people out."

Andy nodded. "You're always trying to make things better for your friends and family. That's a good thing, though. Remember how hard you worked to help Maya figure out which guy was the right boyfriend for her?"

"But she ended up going with a totally different one," I pointed out.

"So what? At least you tried," Andy said. "That's what counts."

"Yeah, I guess you're right. Okay, so what did it say for you?" I asked Maya, wanting to take the focus off me.

She crunched the numbers for a minute, then read the entry and started to giggle. "It said I'd be ideal working in an analytical but artistic environment. Like maybe as an architect or designer."

"I believe that. You'd do a great job designing things," I said to her. "And maybe in the future you can design a car that automatically fixes itself so teenagers won't be killed by their parents for minor accidents."

Andy jumped up, grabbing me by the shoulders. "Wait a minute. I can't believe I didn't think about this before, but I think Bobby's older brother fixes up cars. I bet he could help me out, or at least find someone who can!"

"Yay! See, I told you the answer would come to us if we were patient," Maya said sagely. "Always trust me, young one."

Andy slugged her in the upper arm, causing Maya to grimace in mock pain. "Thanks a lot for the tip, sensei."

"Are we there yet?" I teased Derek in a mock whiny voice. I stepped over a fallen tree limb on the walking path through the park's wooded trail, clinging to his hand as I lagged behind him.

Derek turned back to look at me, shaking his head lightly. "Patience. We're almost there. Just a few more minutes." He slung his mysterious duffel bag over his shoulder and continued forward.

I was glad he'd at least told me we were going to be outside on this Saturday afternoon mystery date he'd planned for us. I was originally planning to wear another one of my new hoochie outfits, but I certainly didn't need bugs or leaves or other outdoor crap falling down my shirt or into my hair. So instead, I had on my favorite jeans, a green T-shirt with a picture of the Beatles on it, and a black baseball cap.

In the back of my mind I kept repeating my secret mantra: *Derek isn't himself right now because of the love spell, so don't be too excited by whatever he does, or you may set yourself up for heartbreak later once the spell wears off.* The worst thing I could do for myself was to start believing this was all real. I could and should be appreciative, but until I'd won him over for good, I had to stay on my guard and not mess anything up.

We walked for what seemed like forever until we stepped into a clearing. The trees opened up, and there was a large field of grass and multicolored flowers in front of us. The sun peeked out from behind the clouds, warming us instantly.

"Derek, this is so pretty!" I exclaimed, squeezing his hand in excitement. My face turned up to the sun as I soaked in the moment.

He tugged me forward. "Come on, we're not done yet."

We walked into the middle of the field, where Derek dropped his duffel bag and started digging through it. After a moment he whipped out a small blanket, just big enough for two to fit on, and spread it over the grass.

"Have a seat," he said. He turned back to the bag and pulled out two food containers, cans of soda, silverware, and a stereo. After plugging his iPod into the stereo, he pressed play. A romantic song by Coldplay came through the speakers.

I swallowed, taking off my hat and sitting down. "I love this song," I whispered. Damn, he was making it hard for me to maintain an impersonal distance. Today's date might be the biggest challenge of my life.

Derek nodded, locking eyes with me. "Yeah, I know."

"How?"

He shrugged casually. "I have my ways. Anyway," he continued, pressing one of the food containers into my hand, "let's eat. I'm starving."

I peeled the lid back, and a waft of deliciousness hit my nose.

"Oh man, meat loaf!" I exclaimed. "I can't believe you can cook, too!"

Derek blushed. "Didn't make it. I enlisted my mom's help. Ya know, 'cause I wanted the food to be edible."

"Well, be sure to thank her for me." I grabbed a fork and began to dig in. My stomach was rumbling, especially after all that walking we did. It was delicious and tender and juicy. I could probably have eaten his plate, too, but decided not to look like a superpig.

Needless to say, we polished off the food in record time. After tossing the containers and silverware back in the duffel bag, we lounged back on the blanket and stared at the sky. Another of my favorite songs came on, this one by The Fray.

My heart sped up. Had he made a mix playlist for me? Geez, Derek didn't believe in doing anything halfway. He sure was pulling out all the stops.

He reached his arm out and tugged me close to his side. I could feel his chest rising and falling. The heat from his muscular body poured into mine, warming me. We kissed for several intense minutes. I stroked his back and shoulders as he rubbed my waist and pressed me against him.

Finally, I pressed one last kiss on the corner of his cheek, then closed my eyes, laying my head on his shoulder. We lay in perfect silence, me cuddled in the crook of his side and my arm flung over his chest. I wanted to relax and fully enjoy the moment, but my mind wouldn't stop spinning. It was so, so tempting to flat-out ask him how he was feeling, if he really liked me for me or if it was the spell. But I already knew the answer, even if he didn't.

I opened my eyes, turned on to my back, and stared at the thick mass of clouds as they slid back in front of the sun.

"You okay?" he asked, turning his head to look at me.

"I'm fine," I said. "I'm just . . . digesting my food." Ugh. Yeah, that was supersexy of me to say, especially after we'd just been making out. Good grief. Talking like that wasn't going to keep him in love with me. It was time to change the subject. "So . . . how about you tell me more about yourself?"

Brilliant idea! If I could find out those little details about his likes and dislikes, maybe I could do some well-tailored wooing of my own. Surely he'd be flattered by whatever I did, right?

"What do you want to know?" he asked me, giving me a crooked grin.

"How about this: We'll do a quick question and answer. Don't think, just answer the questions, okay?"

"Sure, but you have to do it too."

I nodded. "You got it. Okay, favorite movie?"

"*Kill Bill* one and two. Favorite color?"

"Blue," I said. The wind picked up and rustled my hair around. I tucked it behind my ear. "Worst thing you've ever done?"

"Whew," he said, blinking. "Hitting the hard stuff, aren't we?" He paused, thinking. "Okay, I'll be honest. I stole a used CD from one of those exchange stores a few years ago. Not my finest hour, and I regret doing it. Most embarrassing moment?"

God, like I could pick just one. I decided to not admit the whole fiasco when Derek had seen me trying on bikinis in Target, and my mom had shouted to the entire store about my small chest size.

"Maybe seeing my folks getting it on, right there on their bedroom floor? Or how about the time last year I had a rip on the back of my jeans and didn't know it, and my ass cheek hung out for the whole world to see? Or perhaps the time I face-planted while diving for a volleyball in gym," I said, grimacing.

Derek shook his head, chuckling. "You could write a book on disasters."

He had no idea. "Okay," I said, "worst date ever."

"Well," Derek said, turning his face back toward the sky, "I took a girl out last year, and all she did was complain about everything:

She didn't like the restaurant. She thought the movie was awful. She spent the entire evening telling me how terrible her life was and how much she hated most people at school, including my friends."

I cringed. Actually, I didn't like his friends, either. They were snobby and rude. But I decided to keep my mouth shut.

Derek continued, "As you can imagine, that was our first and last date. Anyway, tell me your biggest regret."

The oxygen froze in my lungs. I knew without a doubt what was my biggest regret—knowing that my relationship with Derek would forever be tainted. Not that I could tell him that, though.

I sat up and stared at my feet stretched out in front of me. My good mood had slipped away, again. How could I keep going through this? Having him do these sweet, romantic gestures and not being able to enjoy them properly?

In a low voice I simply said, "Cupid issues." There, that was generic enough. He'd probably think I was talking about the job, not us.

"What do you mean?" he asked, his brows scrunched up.

"I don't want to get into it right now," I hedged.

He sat up and fixed a hard stare on my face. "I thought that was the point of the game. To be honest."

The sky grew dark. I glanced up.

"I think it's going to rain," I said quietly.

Right at that moment the clouds opened up and raindrops began pouring down. We jumped up off the blanket, piling our belongings and all of our trash into the duffel bag as quickly as we could. I crammed the hat back on my head and shivered as big splotches of rain smacked me on the shoulders.

Derek held out the blanket to me. "Wrap up in this to keep you dry," he said. The rain smashed his hair against his head as it beat down harder. Drops of water slid down the angles of his face and plopped onto his shirt.

"But you'll get wet!" I protested. I handed it back to him. "Here, take it."

"Just use it," he said with a sigh, tugging the bag over his shoulder. He moved toward the path. "Let's get back to the car."

I wrapped the blanket around my upper body and hustled after him. We plunged into the woods, brusquely walking along the path. Mud sloshed our feet and peppered my pants legs. I stared at his back, the wet shirt clinging to his broad shoulders. Always the gentleman, he'd sacrificed his own comfort for mine.

It would have been easy to blame the end of the date on the rain. But, deep down, I knew it was my fault, my inability to take him at face value and my discomfort with the secret knowledge I had about him.

And my unwillingness to illuminate that, for fear it meant I would lose him for good.

"Would you like another bowl of chili?" my dad asked Annette, the cop I'd paired Rob up with, at Sunday dinner.

She smiled, rubbing a hand over her stomach as she leaned back in her chair. "Oh my God, I'm stuffed," she said with a laugh. "But thank you! That was killer chili. . . . What did you put in it? Mine never turns out that good."

"Well," Dad said, leaning across the table toward her in a conspiratorial manner, "my secret ingredient is Jack Daniel's. The alcohol cooks out, but it adds a rich flavor that can't be beat."

Whoa.

My dad had never told anyone outside the family what was in his chili. And I mean *never*. He guarded the recipe as if it were a Fort Knox–worthy secret. In fact, according to my mom, he didn't even tell *her* until after he'd proposed. So, Annette must have really made a good impression on him.

Of course, given the kind of women Rob had brought home, it

wasn't too hard for her to stand out above the rest. But even so, she was the best date he'd ever brought around. From the time Annette came through the door, she was smiling, friendly, and responsive to us and, most notably, to Rob.

Plus, she'd helped set the dinner table and complimented my mom on our house.

And not only that, but my brother seemed genuinely smitten with her. I'd never seen him like this before—affectionate and sincere in his attention. Every time she told a joke, he laughed like she was the funniest person he'd ever heard. He'd even jumped up to get a paper towel when she'd spilled a little bit of her drink, insisting on no one else helping.

It would almost be a little gaggy if I hadn't been reveling in the glorious sensation of another happy love match. I fervently hoped they would make it past the two weeks.

Mom carried the empty chili bowls into the kitchen. "Felicity, can you help me clean up?" she hollered into the dining room.

"Sure." I grabbed the rest of the dirty dishes and went into the kitchen after her, loading up the dishwasher. "So, Annette seems nice," I offered, wanting to see Mom's opinion of my love match for Rob. I knew I could count on her to be honest.

Mom, who was putting the leftover chili into the fridge, nodded in agreement. "I like her. This girl seems quite different from others he's brought home."

"Well, it helps that she's fully dressed. And that she's not trying to date Dad," I said, laughing.

She closed the fridge door. "Yeah, that's always a relief. I'm tired of having to fight for him," she joked. "Truthfully, though, I've never seen your brother fall this hard for a girl before. She'd better treat him right."

Peals of laughter from Dad, Rob, and Annette came from the dining room.

"Mr. Walker, you're hilarious!" I heard Annette say. "Rob, you didn't tell me your dad was so funny. I can see where you get your great sense of humor from."

"So, does she get your official seal of approval?" I asked Mom.

Head cocked toward the dining room, she nodded. "Absolutely."

"She gets mine, too," I said quietly, with a smile. I didn't always like my brother, but he deserved to be with someone who made him happy. And it made me feel good to find a girl like that for him.

Chapter 12

Riding high on my brilliant matchmaking, I ran upstairs once Rob and Annette had left and grabbed my LoveLine 3000. I fired it up, randomly picking one of the names on my list: Randall Schlemming.

I pulled up his profile:

Name: Randall Schlemming

Age: 18

Interests: Filmmaking. Quirky postmodern art galleries. Loves to talk about hot topics to people in class.

Smart guy.

Style: Artsy Individualist

I heard him say that after graduation he was hoping to move to California and become a movie director. He needed to be matched to someone who was ambitious and outgoing to match his strong personality.

I scrolled through my list, finding two different girls who seemed like they might work well. Janie was a writer who had won some regional writing contests. The fact that she was competitive and believed in perfecting her craft would certainly appeal to someone like Randall.

On the other hand, Laura was truly an artiste, into action painting and performance art. She, too, wanted to move to California and be a part of some artistic movement when she graduated.

So, which girl was the right choice?

I studied them both for a few seconds, overwhelmed and unable to select. My heart rate sped up, and my lips started to tingle as a wave of dizziness swept over me. What if neither one of these girls was right for Randall—was I being too superficial in my match-making again?

Maybe I should just pick one and give it a try. I chose Janie and added her and Randall to my love-matching e-mail.

Press send, I told myself.

But I couldn't do it.

There was definitely something wrong with me. Where was my enthusiasm, my courage from ten minutes ago? Why had it vanished on me?

I laid my PDA on my nightstand and draped myself across my bed, burying my face in my pillow. This was so, so not good. How could I be a cupid if I couldn't even make any matches? I mean, hello—that was the purpose of my job.

What was I going to do?

Hey, maybe I could talk to Derek about it.

I reached over to grab my phone, then stopped. Things were a little awkward with us right now after our date yesterday afternoon, and this wasn't going to help me look appealing to him. Besides, after boasting so hard that I was kicking butt with my list, it would be lame to say, "Hey, I take it back. I suck at this, and I'm stuck."

Just as I went to pull my hand away from the receiver, the phone rang. A startled shiver ran across my skin. Was Derek calling me?

I lifted the phone and checked the caller ID—nope, it was Maya.

"Can you come over?" she whispered after we said our hellos.

"My dad's on his way here to meet with my mom, and I need some moral support."

I sat up, sucking in a quick, nervous breath. "Absolutely. I'm on my way."

After we hung up, I threw on my tennis shoes and headed to Maya's house, fretting the whole way as I paced the sidewalk. Would our attempt at helping Mrs. Takahashi make herself over work?

Finally I got to the front door. Before I could even knock, the door was flung open, and Maya tugged me inside without saying a word, leading me up to her room.

"Thanks for coming," she finally said, hugging me quickly. When we reached her room at the top of the stairs, we left her bedroom door open so we could hear what was going on down in the living room, then perched on the edge of her bed. "I just got really nervous and started to feel sick, and I figured this would be easier if you were here."

"I wouldn't be anywhere else," I said. "Is Andy coming, too?"

She shook her head. "She's at work right now, and I didn't want to bother her there. Anyway—"

Maya stopped when we heard the front door open. She gripped

my hand tightly. "Oh God, he's here!" she whispered, her eyes wide. "He hasn't seen my mom yet. I hope he's surprised!"

"Me too," I said, trying to ignore the shooting pain going up my arm from her death grip. "I'm sure he'll be floored."

Mrs. Takahashi, who I guess had been in the kitchen, came into the living room. "Come on in," she said, her voice soft and warm. "I'm glad you could make it. Here, let me take your coat."

I saw Maya swallow and lean toward the door, her body tense.

The warm, delicious smell of Japanese food wafted up to the room. As part of our plan, Maya's mom had made her husband a traditional dinner, knowing he had a soft spot for her cooking.

"I'm sorry; I can't stay long," Maya's dad said in his typical low, rumbling voice.

Silence.

"But I thought you were staying for dinner," Mrs. Takahashi said. "I thought we were going to talk."

Maya sucked in a quick breath, turning her frantic eyes to me. "He's not staying? That wasn't part of the plan. And he hasn't commented on my mom's looks at all."

I shrugged helplessly, my heart sinking. This wasn't going well, and I had a bad feeling that they weren't going to make amends tonight, regardless of how nice she looked or how confident she tried to seem.

"I'm sorry," Mr. Takahashi repeated.

We heard some papers rustling. Then more silence.

"What's going on?" Maya whispered to me, the line between her brows deep. "Why aren't they talking?"

"I didn't realize . . . you were actually going to go through with this." Mrs. Takahashi's voice was quiet, unemotional. "You already have papers drawn up?"

Mr. Takahashi cleared his throat. "I need to go. I'll have my attorney contact you tomorrow, okay?"

The door closed.

Maya and I stared at each other in horror. I mean, what could I possibly say to make anyone feel better?

"I should . . . go downstairs." Maya rose from the bed and went out of her room, me following right behind.

Mrs. Takahashi stood in the living room, staring at the front door. Her back was ramrod straight, and she clutched the divorce papers in her hand.

I opened my mouth to speak, then decided to stay silent.

Maya, though, ran over and hugged her mom tightly, tears

springing to her eyes. "I'm sorry, Mom," she said. "I'm sorry we let you down."

"You didn't do anything wrong," Mrs. Takahashi said, her voice choked. She patted Maya's back. "It just wasn't meant to be, I guess."

"Maybe we can try something else," I offered.

She shook her head sadly. "No, I think I'm done. I'm better off accepting the reality of this situation than chasing a dream."

After a moment of silence I decided to let the two of them have some private time together.

"I'll catch you at school, okay, Maya?" I said, easing toward the front door.

She gave a slow nod, too choked up to speak.

Once I'd closed the door behind me, I let the tears I'd been fighting slide down my cheeks.

How awful! I couldn't believe the dinner had gone that badly. None of us had expected it to end that way.

Mrs. Takahashi's words haunted me, echoing round and round in my head. Was she right? Was true love just a dream?

As I sludged my way back home, I thought of all the failed couples I'd paired since I'd become a matchmaker, and of all the love-spelled pairs that could so easily break up when their spells wore off.

And then I thought of my own tentative match with Derek, a spell that would end in three days. Would we make it past then?

We had to. We just *had* to. Or I didn't know what I was going to do.

I opened the front door.

"Oh, Felicity," Mom hollered from the kitchen, "is that you? Can you help me with the laundry?"

"Sure," I replied, trying not to groan.

Oh, well . . . maybe sorting lights and darks would help get my mind off all the bad stuff going on right now.

In the basement I got the first load of laundry started, then went up to my room as quietly as I could before Mom could assign me another task. I locked my door behind me, booted up my computer, and logged on to my blog, setting the entry to private diary. I needed to spill all of these crazy emotions out of me.

Everything is just chaos. Why can't I seem to make love go right for anyone—including myself?

Being matched up with Derek should probably have been a good thing. Instead, I'm paranoid and studying his every move . . . and my own, wondering if I'm going to accidentally do something to push him away from me. Every time I'm around him, I'm awkward and end up making things a little crappier than before.

And just as bad, I seem to have lost my matchmaking mojo. What's the deal with that? I try to pair people up, but I freeze. I just can't make myself send the e-mails.

My phone rang. The caller ID showed it was Derek.

Heart racing, I picked it up. "Hello?"

"Hey," he said. "I tried to call earlier, but your mom said you were out. How was your day?"

"Well . . . things are going kind of bad for Maya right now, so I went over to hang out with her," I answered slowly. I didn't feel like trying to be Miss Mysterious, so I let the act go for the night.

"You're a good friend to her. I'm sure she appreciated it."

His voice sounded so warm, I almost wanted to cry. After what had happened with Mr. and Mrs. Takahashi, I was beyond glad to talk to him. And to see that he wasn't being supercold because of the way yesterday afternoon's date ended.

"So, how are things going at your house?" I asked, hoping my voice didn't give away my angst.

"Not bad. My mom's stomach is getting bigger every day. She says she can tell this baby's gonna be a soccer player because he's kicking her constantly. You can even see his foot pressing against her stomach. It's weird." He laughed. "Just what we need—another sports nut in the house."

"Felicity!" Mom's voice echoed all the way into my room. "I need your help straightening the pantry and shelves in the kitchen."

I groaned. "Gotta go. The House Nazi strikes again, and she's beckoning me to do more slave work."

"Okay, I'll see ya tomorrow morning outside of school," Derek said. I could hear the grin in his voice.

We hung up, and I logged off my PC as well, trying to hold on to a bit of Derek's warmth. Surely I wasn't just chasing a dream . . . right?

Chapter 13

T-minus two days and counting until the cupid spell would wear off of me and Derek.

I stood on the front steps of school and scoured the grounds with my eyes, waiting for him to show up. I'd dressed to kill today, wearing another of the new outfits I'd bought with my cupid earnings: a pair of low-rise jeans, ballet flats, and a fabulous red top.

Confidence. Self-assurance. Those were my mantras for the day, the subtle messages I'd replayed in my brain over and over to remind myself of the ultimate goal: keeping Derek past Wednesday. Bonus: This might also help me with my other goal, which was to get my sorry hiney back into matchmaking.

After lying awake for hours in bed last night, I'd finally gotten up and sneaked downstairs to watch a movie, hoping to take my mind off all the turmoil. There wasn't much on the boob tube at the time except for a bad infomercial, about some "magical" exercise product that could flatten your abs in ten seconds a day, and a black-and-white Katharine Hepburn movie. I opted for the latter.

Surprisingly, I found myself giggling at her antics, as well as admiring her. She was tall, sassy, and confident, and she owned it. No wonder she'd drawn the male lead to her . . . how could he resist?

So, I'd decided to not dwell on my panic and fears for the next couple of days, but to make a genuine attempt to enjoy the time I had with Derek. I'd give him good memories of me instead of acting like a total insecure freakshow, and surely that would make it hard for him to walk away.

I hoped.

"Hi, Felicity," Derek whispered in my ear from behind me, his soft breath tickling my neck.

I spun around, heart leaping into my throat. "Hi, yourself," I answered, giving him as big of a smile as I could manage. He needed to see how much I loved his company. His laughter. *Him.*

"Sorry I'm a little late." The sunlight hit his hair, bathing it in a bright gold. He looked like a Greek god.

Trying not to swoon at his feet, I said, "No big deal at all. I was happy to wait for you." Crap, I didn't mean to sound so needy or desperate.

Back off, Felicity, I ordered myself. *Remember the plan.*

I threaded my fingers through his and walked through the school's front doors, trying to figure out my next move. What witty thing could I say to show him I was the most confident, self-assured girl at Greenville High?

"So, how did your evening go?" Derek asked before I could bring up a discussion topic, his face eager as he peered over at me. His thumb slowly swirled against my skin of my palm. "I got the last chunk of my matches done last night. Those tables and charts in the manual were invaluable."

Aw man, it looked like I was totally going to lose the bet. I should have known he'd want to talk about this. And I couldn't believe he'd actually finished his whole list.

The guy was determined, for sure.

"Oh, that's fantastic!" I said. Maybe my praise and enthusiasm about his accomplishments would deter him from pressing me further about my own performance. I squeezed his hand, hoping some of his matchmaking mojo would rub off on me. "You're doing so well at this. Janet's going to be impressed."

"Thanks. So did you finish—" He stopped himself midsentence and turned his attention to his football-jock friend Toby Brown, who was barreling down the hallway toward us. "Hey, man!"

"Derek!" Toby hollered as he slapped him on the back. Everything Toby said was at maximum volume, which got to be really annoying about five seconds into him talking. Maybe he should get his ears checked or something. "Dude, you gotta come to my locker. I have the funniest picture in there—it's so gross." He grabbed Derek's upper arm and tugged him away, totally ignoring me.

Derek paused, turning to look at me. "You coming?"

Toby stopped, his upper lip curling as he turned my way. Yeah, he totally didn't want me there—it was written all over his face.

"What are you guys going to look at?" I asked.

"You probably wouldn't be interested. It's a guy thing," Toby answered, then turned his attention back to Derek.

Suck. I'd been looking forward to having some extra time with Derek this morning, but it was apparent he wanted to go hang with his friends, too. No way, though, did I want to spend more than point-five seconds in their company. I'd had enough of that at Starbucks a few nights ago, thank you very much.

Besides, secure girlfriends didn't cling to their guys like they knew they were going to up and leave any second, right? And just as important, they didn't come between a guy and his friends. Derek never did that to me, and I wanted to give him the same respect.

I gave a casual wave to them both. Trying to sound like my heart wasn't slamming in my chest, I said, "Nah, you two go on. I gotta run to class early, anyway."

"Okay, I'll catch you later!" Derek said with a big smile, then turned and left.

Hmmm. Though I'd wanted to show him how self-confident I could be, pretending like being dissed by his friends didn't hurt my feelings wasn't what I'd intended. But lately that kind of thing was happening more and more. Was it possible they were trying to lure him away from me?

It's not like that was unheard of. I distinctly remembered how often the friends of Marisa, a girl I'd matchmade, tried to get her to dump her boyfriend DeShawn. She'd stuck by her guns, though, and had refused to give him up.

Would Derek do the same for me?

I headed toward English class, running the concept through my head. As much as I wanted to be indignant, I understood how influential friends could be in each other's lives. I weighed the opinions of Andy and Maya very heavily. If they'd told me to stay away from Derek, would I have listened to them?

Well, anyway, it was a moot point. My friends would only say that if he were a jerk. And he wasn't.

But did Derek's friends have a problem with *me*?

Maybe I'd done something accidentally to insult them, and now they didn't think I was good enough for him. Or maybe they were just big jerks. Who knew? I'd just have to be extra careful around them and not give them any new reason to dislike me.

Fortunately, the bell to start the day interrupted my thoughts. I made my way to my desk and sat down beside Maya, who was already in class.

Mrs. Kendel lingered by the door for a minute or so, then closed it, thumping her way to the front of class. "I graded your papers," she said, her lips pursed. "Not. Good. I was very disappointed in the quality of your narratives."

My stomach sank. Was she talking about mine? Granted, I'd been working my butt off with matchmaking and trying to keep

Derek . . . but something told me Mrs. Kendel wouldn't understand that, or care.

Well, so much for oozing self-confidence. With each passing second, I got more and more insecure.

Come on! I ordered myself. My fluctuating feelings were getting out of control. I felt like everything was spiraling away from me—could that be part of the reason I was having a hard time making matches?

Mrs. Kendel wandered up and down the aisles, handing back our papers. She put them facedown on our desks. When she got to me, she plopped the paper down and moved on.

I stared at the back of it, almost afraid to flip it over.

Maya nudged me in the side. "What did you get?" she asked, her voice low.

With a quick movement I turned the paper faceup. And then groaned, wanting to thunk my head on the desktop.

"A C-minus," I whispered back.

Oh joy, Mrs. Kendel had even written a note at the top: *Come see me after class.* Gee, that sounded promising. Maybe she wanted to praise me for having the best C-minus paper she'd ever graded. Yeah, I'm sure.

Somehow I managed to fake my way through the rest of class like I was listening to everything she said. In reality, I wanted to run back home, jump in bed, and pretend like this day hadn't started yet.

But one good thing did come out of the period—when thinking about my plans for the evening, I'd realized that Janet was the perfect person for me to talk to about my cupid matchmaking problems in my meeting with her tonight. While I wasn't crazy about 'fessing up, I knew as soon as she saw my PDA that my lack of matches would be obvious.

Therefore, I figured I could approach her and ask for some advice. A little proactivity on my part couldn't hurt.

The bell rang. I told Maya I'd meet her at lunch and then slowly made my way to the front of the classroom, feeling like I was walking to my own funeral.

And, in a way, I was. Mom was going to kill me for getting a C-minus on my paper. I just hoped she didn't take her wrath out on me in a way that would affect prom.

"Miss Walker," Mrs. Kendel said, staring up at me from her chair with arms crossed over her ample chest. "I'm very disappointed in the quality of your paper. I expected better from you. You're one of my best students in class."

Yowch. Mrs. Kendel didn't beat around the bush or anything, did she?

Then the second part of her words hit me like a brick in the face—she considered *me* one of her best students?

"*R-Really?*" I sputtered. Color me floored. Praise from Mrs. Kendel was a rare occurrence, indeed.

"You always give smart, thoughtful answers on the assignments, but this narrative isn't quite up to your standards. It lacks the focus and depth I'd have expected. But I think you knew that already, didn't you?" She gave me a pointed look with her small, steely eyes, one eyebrow lifted.

I swallowed hard and gave a small nod.

Ziiiing. Mrs. Kendel had no idea how accurately she'd nailed the problem I'd been struggling with for almost two weeks . . . and my relationship woes weren't even what she was addressing! Too weird.

"Do you have any ideas about how I can make sure my papers have focus and depth?" I asked.

She scratched her chin, leaning back in her chair. "Well, I recommend outlining exactly whatever it is you want to achieve in your paper. Break it down in simple language so you stay on track, but don't get overwhelmed by whatever you're facing."

"Okay, I can do that."

"Slow and steady works well. And stick close to your main purpose—that's the important part." She flipped through a big-ass pile of papers on the corner. "Here," she said, thrusting a handout at me. "This'll give you tips on how to outline and draft a paper."

Actually, the idea had merit not only in my English class but also in real life. Maybe instead of wandering around and grasping at straws trying to come up with a billion different plans regarding Derek and my matchmaking woes, I should focus on one solid idea and follow it through.

"I'll give that a try—on the next paper, I mean," I said awkwardly, clutching the outline handout.

"Luckily, this shouldn't affect your grade too much. But don't start sliding downhill," she warned, wagging a finger at me. "It's much easier to drop a grade level than it is to raise it, you know."

"Okay." I made the "cross my heart" gesture.

She scrawled a note out for me, permitting me to be late to American history since we'd talked past the bell, and then sent me on my way.

°   °   °

That evening at work, during my regular meeting with Janet, I sat in the chair across from her desk and unloaded my matchmaking problems. To her credit, she didn't make a sound, letting me spill the beans about my worries and panic for several minutes.

"And I just don't know how to get my matchmaking mojo back," I said in summary. "Do you know what I can do?"

Janet nodded her head knowingly, folding her hands on the smooth surface of her desk. "Oh, so you got cupid's block."

"Huh?"

"Cupid's block. Like writer's block, but instead of being blocked while writing a novel, you're blocked while making matches. It's very common among first-year cupids," Janet said, her voice smooth and even. "Happens to most of us."

A small, sullen part of me bet that Derek would be among the small percentage of those who were never afflicted. But since that was uncharitable and totally jealous of me, I quieted that part down.

"Have you ever gotten it?" I asked.

"I did, yes." She paused. "I'd only been a cupid for six months at the time. I quit the company for a full year because of it."

"Whoa, really? What happened?" Maybe hearing her experience would help me unblock myself—er, so to speak.

She sighed, rubbing a hand along the back of her neck. "Oh, it was a long time ago, and I was very insecure and nervous. I'd made several matches that had fallen apart—very publicly—and I was mortified when those celebrity couples split up. One of the relationships ended in a tragedy. I don't want to go into details, but needless to say, it wasn't good."

Wow. I guess matchmaking teens wasn't nearly as bad or pressure-filled as what Janet had gone through. At least I wasn't making celebrity matches!

"After that, I couldn't seem to make any more couples," she went on. "No matter how hard I tried, I was petrified that they'd end up hating each other and breaking up after the spell wore off. So, I turned in my bow and arrow and gave up the business." She propped her chin up with her hands, a small, wistful smile on her face. "I actually went to beauty school, thinking I'd change careers and leave matchmaking behind me."

"But you didn't. You came back."

"Yes, I came back. It was in my blood, you see." She placed her hands in her lap. "I just had to take time to learn some tricks for getting over my cupid's block."

"Such as?" I leaned forward, eager to take mental notes.

"The first thing I had to do was relax."

I drooped my upper body against the back of my chair. "Okay, I'm there."

She chuckled. "I mean, relax my attitude, though I guess relaxing your physical self can help too. It's so easy to get caught up in the madness of matchmaking and blow it out of proportion, but remember that love is only one aspect of someone's life. Not everyone is going to fall in love with each other. And even if they do, that doesn't mean that they'll stay in love forever."

I nodded in agreement, thinking about poor Mrs. Takahashi's broken marriage. And about my own precarious match with Derek. "No kidding. It's so scary thinking that love can end at any time."

"Well, if I kept my purpose in mind," she continued, "then I was golden. My job was to help people find the opportunity for love as best as I could."

I listened to her words, replaying them in my head a couple of times. The opportunity for love. Okay, I could do that. After all, it sounded like a lot less pressure than my current motto, which was more like, *Don't screw up and matchmake the wrong people together, idiot!*

"I'm afraid to make mistakes," I admitted sheepishly.

"And that's part of the reason why you have cupid's block.

Being a matchmaker is 'divine work,' if you will. Don't forget that you're human, though, just like everyone else. Nothing we do is going to be perfect. Love certainly isn't perfect—it's messy and crazy and fun and scary. But would we have it any other way?"

The tension in my shoulders seeped away for real this time, and I let her soothing words wash over me. Janet was surprisingly easy to talk to about this. I only wish I'd come to her sooner.

"It'll also help if you try to keep from getting personally involved with your subjects," she continued, her eyes suddenly squinting and staring at me. "I'm guessing this is the other issue affecting you, am I right?"

"Well, it's hard not to," I replied, fighting the edge of defensiveness that slowly crept into my voice. "A lot of them are my friends. I go to school with them. It's natural to want to make the best matches I possibly can."

"Of course you do. That's why I chose you and Derek to work at your school, because you two best understand what your fellow students need in a relationship. But when you're matchmaking, you need to put on your business face, not your friend face." She paused. "Understand what I mean? You have to learn how to create a wall within yourself, so to speak, to be an effective matchmaker."

Ugh. Janet had a good point. It was hard to stay objective when matchmaking people you knew—or who were your best friends. That's why I'd chosen someone I didn't know as my very first match. Maybe I'd gotten too far away from this principle over time, and it was causing me trouble now.

I sighed, squirming in my seat. Man, I wished this job was easier sometimes. "Okay, I'll try."

"If you need help, I'm sure Derek would be more than happy to split the rest of your matches with you," Janet said, her lips parting in a sly smile.

He probably would. There was no way I was going to ask him that, though. I had some scraps of pride left, and handing over my workload to him wasn't going to help me feel better. But I *could* work with him tonight to encourage me to get back on track, and to get his opinion on matches. "Thanks, but I'd rather finish it myself."

"I understand. Okay, why don't you hand over your PDA so I can sync it with the computer? Then we can get you out of here and back to making matches."

At that moment I felt the sudden urge to blurt out that I knew she'd matchmade me and Derek—partly to see if she had any advice on how I could handle it, and partly to see what she'd say about it.

I started to open my mouth but then closed it again. She might get pissed that I was looking through stuff on her desk. And I didn't want to get on her bad side, especially since I'd been screwing up a lot lately. Something told me not to push it with her.

No, this was something I was going to have to deal with myself, just like any other paired-up person who had been hit by Cupid's dart. Or e-mail. Or whatever crazy method she'd used on us.

I wordlessly handed over my PDA. She synced it, and I left, focusing on Janet's advice on the drive home. She was absolutely right about what my problem was and how I could get myself back on the right track for matchmaking.

Now I needed to muster the courage to take her counsel and push past my cupid's block, once and for all.

Chapter 14

"Your room isn't quite what I'd expected it to be," I said to Derek later that evening. I glanced around, a little in shock. Actually, I wasn't sure what I'd thought it would look like, but it wasn't as nice as this.

There were a couple of framed sports posters hanging on the wall in addition to the classic art pieces, like a print of Salvador Dali's melting clocks. The bed was immaculately made and covered with a dark brown comforter. Actually, the whole room was spotless—not an errant sock in sight. Even underneath his bed was clean.

"My mom would kill to have a child like you," I continued with a laugh.

He shook his head, then gestured toward the bed. "Yeah, I like a clean room. That's my type A coming out. So, have a seat." He walked to his door and swung it wide open. "House rules," he said with a chagrined smile.

"No problem. I'm not even allowed to have guys in my room," I explained as I sat down. I pulled my LoveLine 3000 out of my purse and placed it on my lap. "So, you're a step ahead of me." The House Nazi seemed to think if I were left alone with a boy in my bedroom, his sperm would magically travel through his pants and impregnate me, even if we weren't doing anything sexual.

Derek sat down beside me. "So, what's going on? Did your cupid meeting with Janet go okay? You didn't say too much in your phone call."

It took me a moment to answer him. Mostly because I was very, very aware of the fact that Derek and I were alone in his bedroom, and I suddenly didn't want to talk about work crap, which was my original plan for meeting with him. Instead, I wanted for him to grab me and plant a whopper of a kiss right on my lips. And maybe a few on my neck too.

Oy. If I were honest with myself, I guess I could kinda understand now why my mom was trying to avoid this very scenario at our house. Not that I was gonna rip my clothes off and throw myself at him (no babies for me, thank you very much), but the feelings were still quite potent.

I shook off these thoughts and tried to focus on the conversation. "Um, the meeting went fine." I paused, realizing I was about to concede utter defeat in the cupid arena and therefore acknowledge that Derek was better than me. Sigh. "I still have a bunch of matches to make, though, and I'm having problems getting them done."

"And you need me to do them for you? Sure!" Derek went to grab my PDA.

"No!" I shouted.

He froze, eyes wide in shock.

Idiot! I realized how badly that had to sound, both to him and to his family in the rest of the house.

"I, uh, think the answer to that question is five point two," I continued in a loud voice. Then I whispered, "Sorry. I didn't want your parents thinking something bad was happening up here." I paused. "I didn't meant to blurt that out like that. All I need is some advice on pairing up the rest of my couples. I can totally still do them myself."

He chuckled lightly and moved his hand away. "Okay. So what's going on?"

Briefly, I filled him in on my cupid's block, making sure to mention how Janet said it was very common. As I talked, Derek listened intently.

"So, now I still have these couples left, but I'm a little scared to do it. I can't afford to mess up any more lives."

He nodded. "Okay, I think I get it. Let's take it slowly and focus on one person at a time. When I feel overwhelmed, it helps if I look at things in smaller chunks."

"I can do that," I said. Yeah, it sucked that I probably looked really doofy to Derek right now because of this cupid's block, but this wasn't just about me. I had to get these people paired up, so I was checking my ego at the door was for the greater good. I turned on my PDA and found my list. "Here's the original list of people, showing who I've paired up so far and who is left," I said.

He took it from my hands, scrolling down. "Hmmm. I see. Okay. I'm a little surprised you paired Tina with Martin. I figured she'd be perfect for Riley, who is still on your list. What compatibilities did you have for Tina and Martin?"

My cheeks flamed. I forced myself to bite my tongue. *He's trying to help. He's trying to help,* I told myself in my head over and over again.

"Actually, I'd rather focus on the couples I haven't worked on yet," I said, my voice shaky. I cleared my throat. "Besides, I've seen Tina and Martin flirting with each other before, in addition to other things."

My tone must have been edgier than I intended because his lips pinched for the quickest of seconds. "Got it." He turned his attention back to the PDA. "Okay, so let's start with Riley then, since he's still single."

I dug into my purse and whipped out the small notebook I'd brought with me, ready to jot down our ideas. "Sounds like a plan. I had a hard time figuring out who would work well with him, because he's kind of . . ." I paused, trying to find a gentle way to say he was a loudmouth who loved attention.

"He's very outgoing," Derek suggested, ever tactful as usual.

I grinned. "Nice way to word it. Anyway, most of the girls left on the list don't feel to me like they'd be the right match for him."

"So, what results did you get from the charts?"

I knew he'd eventually ask that, so I gave a noncommittal shrug and stated my preplanned answer (read: lie). "Well, the results were inconclusive," I said. I already felt stupid enough needing Derek's help, and I sure didn't want to go down the "charts" road again. "That's why I'm here, talking to you."

He blinked. "Huh? How can they be inconclusive? I've never had that happen before—is that even possible?"

I gritted my teeth. "Derek, why do you always bring up the charts? Not everything in this job can be done through mathematical formulas. At least, not for us lowly cupids who can't seem to make them work right." I swallowed, more than a little surprised at the strength of words that came out of me.

Evidently he was too. His back stiffened. "And what does that mean?"

"It means I want help, not to be referred to the stupid manual. I want to talk to you about this and bounce ideas." My breath was coming out fast, and I struggled to keep my voice low.

"Fine," Derek said, his voice strangely flat. "But I don't see the point in outright ignoring the charts and graphs. Have you even given them a fair try?"

God, did I have to spell it out? Was he going to make me state out loud that I was a grade-A moron?

I stood and started pacing his room. "Yes, okay? I did try them.

They just don't work for me. There's no one right or wrong way to do the matches, you know."

"Maybe if you'd tried to use them a little bit more, things wouldn't be so crazy right now at school," he said quietly.

Ouch.

I reeled back, almost like I'd been physically hit. I turned to face him, staring into his hooded eyes and perfect face. "Maybe *you* should get off your high horse. You don't know everything." All of the dark words that had been building up in me over the past couple of weeks spilled out, and I couldn't stop myself from speaking. "You have to be the best at everything you do. The most wonderful son. The most gifted at art. The smartest guy in school. The best football player we've ever had. The most thoughtful boyfriend a girl could ask for. The prime example of a high school matchmaker. No one else can even come close to your achievements because you've already beaten them to it."

He rose and stood in front of me, his face coldly staring into mine. "Is that really how you feel? Be honest with me. For once."

I nodded, because it was true. And yet it wasn't. I knew Derek wasn't doing all of those things to spite me or anything. But I was angry and hurt and tired of feeling like a moron around him. Why did he have to be the best at everything? Why was I always lagging behind?

Derek crossed his arms. "Wait a minute. I see what's going on here. This isn't about me. It's about you and your feelings of insecurity."

I swallowed. He'd nailed it. Of course. "Oh, and now you're the best amateur psychologist around, too. Gosh, Derek, however do you find time to do it all?" I grabbed my stuff off his bed, crammed them into my purse, and turned toward the door. "I'm just gonna go home and think about how unworthy I am to be with you."

With those parting words, I left.

I woke up the next morning feeling like my face had been smashed with a mallet. My eyes were so puffy from crying all night that I could barely see. How did everything go so horribly wrong? What was it about Derek that brought out the absolute worst parts of me? I hated feeling like a loser all the time around him, knowing he was so talented and smart and special. It was hard to feel like I deserved him.

All the mean words I said to him echoed in my head. God, I was so nasty. He'd wanted me to speak the truth. And boy, had I given it to him, in spades.

I sighed and sat up, shuffling my way to the bathroom. Once

there, I splashed about a million gallons of water on my face, trying to reduce the swelling. I was going to look like a train wreck at school today, but hopefully I could reduce the damage through some strategic makeup application.

My stomach lurched as I thought about Derek. What should I say to him at school? What would he say to me? Today was our last day of being under the spell, and I highly suspected that I'd blown it last night. He probably wouldn't speak to me now, and our relationship would fizzle out before it even could have for-real begun.

I dressed quickly, skipped breakfast, and headed right to school. My heart raced the entire time. Would he be waiting for me outside? Would he want to talk? Would I be the first person in the world to be dumped before the spell even wore off?

This was ridiculous. I forced those questions out of my head. He most likely would not be waiting for me this morning. But I could take time today to talk to Maya and Andy to see what they thought I could do. I had to be generic, of course, and not mention the cupid angle. But I could still give them the gist of the situation. I'd been too stressed and tearful to even call them last night, wanting to get some perspective before I dumped everything on them. So I was eager to see them today.

I headed to the front of the school, staring at the steps. The makeup had covered some of my blotchiness, but not all. So the less eye contact I made with people, the better.

A hand reached out and tapped me on the shoulder. It was Adele, the girl in my English class I'd matchmade who had made out with her new boyfriend in front of all of us. "Have you seen it?" she asked me.

"Seen what?"

"Oh my God, you haven't seen it yet," she whispered. A huge grin broke out on her face. "Just wait. Eeh! I'm going to come inside with you."

I blinked, offering her a watery grin. "I have no idea what you're talking about, but okay." She and I weren't BFFs or anything, but we were on friendly terms. I was a little surprised to see her come up and talk to me, though. Maybe the love spell I'd done on her had made her more outgoing.

"Felicity!" Maya said in front of me, running down the top half of the stairs toward me. "Wow, you have to come inside. Come in!"

"What's going on?" Things were Twilight-Zone crazy here this morning. Why did everyone want so badly for me go into the building?

"Just come and see," Maya said, her eyes wide.

As I ascended the stairs, I noticed people were staring at me, whispering fervently. I felt like I was going to throw up. What was all this? Was I in trouble? No, that couldn't be it—Maya wouldn't let me walk into the lion's den unprepared.

The doors were pulled open for me, and I stepped inside the front lobby. Right away I saw pillars set up with various sculptures. Paintings and drawings of all shapes and sizes adorned the wall.

Duh, the art show. With all the drama in my life lately, I'd completely forgotten. I'd even carried a couple of the paintings to the teacher's lounge with Derek—that was when we'd busted Mr. Wiley and Brenda going at it on the couch.

Then I froze. On the left wall there was a huge framed mosaic that had to be almost five feet tall.

It was an image of me.

The sounds of the hallway faded away from me, and the only thing I could hear was a rushing sound in my ears. I stepped toward the mosaic, staring in shock and disbelief. It was me, sitting outside of school on a bench, staring off into space. The sunlight poured onto my hair, and my eyes sparkled. There was a slightly mysterious smile curving my lips.

I looked . . . beautiful.

The bottom right corner signature confirmed my suspicions. Derek had created this picture and entered it in the art show.

"Felicity! Felicity!" Maya's voice penetrated my fog. "Oh my God, isn't it amazing? He must have worked forever on this piece."

"I can't stop staring at it," Adele said, sighing happily.

"It's amazing," I replied, my tongue thick. "He's really gifted."

The most gifted at art. My words to Derek last night echoed back to me. I felt like a huge, huge ass.

What was wrong with me? Why had I lashed out at him so harshly over my own personal issues? I knew before I dated him that he was supertalented. It was one of the things about him that I'd fallen in love with. He wasn't just a meathead like other guys at school—he had depth, substance, real talent. Which was why he was so freaking popular at school and so many people loved him.

And I'd rubbed all of that in his face as if it were a flaw instead of something to be proud of.

I sighed. Still, that didn't take away the fact that this had obviously been a love-spell-induced portrait. It was too perfect, too stunning, too carefully crafted to be otherwise.

God, why couldn't things be normal in my life, just for once? A beautiful image of me was here in the hallway, proclaiming Derek's love for all to see. But could I enjoy it? No. I knew our relationship was a sham. Plus, we'd had that horrible fight last night, which made things all the worse.

Maya snapped a pic of the mosaic with her cell phone. "This way we can enjoy it whenever we're not near this hallway to see it in person."

Adele, Maya, and I headed to first period. Mike jumped out of his seat and gave Adele a big hug, which was a bittersweet sort of feeling for me. I was happy to see their relationship going well but wishing mine would get some breaks.

Of course, I didn't focus on a single word Mrs. Kendel said the entire time. Instead, I thought about what I'd say when I saw Derek in art class . . . or if I happened to see him in the hallways earlier.

First, I'd apologize for our fight last night. And Derek being Derek, he'd probably apologize, too. He was too much of a gentleman not to. Then I'd thank him for the mosaic and ask if I could keep it when the art show was over. That way, even if he and I ended up splitting up (my throat closed up every time I thought this), I could have something to remember him by.

My stomach was a total mess all day. I didn't even eat lunch, just picked at my sandwich like a bird. Instead, Maya and Andy kept looking at Maya's cell pic of the mosaic and gushing over how great of a job Derek did in rendering me. I nodded and smiled in all the right places, but on the inside I felt hollow and tired. This wasn't the time to ruin everyone's good mood and go on and on about how he and I had fought last night. I'd just talk to them later.

It didn't help that I hadn't heard a word about Derek, and no one else had seen him at all today.

Art class finally came and went. Unfortunately, Derek was nowhere to be found—he'd called in sick. I should have known he wouldn't come. Of course. He was obviously fully aware the art show was going on and didn't want to see me.

But I could call him later today from Bobby's house, since I was going with Andy as moral support while she met with Bobby's car-mechanic brother. I knew Andy would let me borrow her cell for a few minutes.

Yes, I resolved to make things right. I'd apologize to him for the harsh words I'd said and thank him profusely for the mosaic. It was the least I could do.

What would happen after that was anyone's guess.

Chapter 15

"Can you fix it?" Andy's eyes were small and filled with fear as she watched George, Bobby's car-fixer-upper brother who was currently crouched in front of the Porsche's bumper, studying the damage.

I rubbed her back, trying to give her a little comfort, and mentally crossed my fingers that George could repair the damage.

He stood and, with a thick hand covered in dirt and grime, scratched his chin that bristled with short, coarse, black hairs. Surprisingly, he looked a good fifteen years older than Bobby, which made me suspect their parents were a lot older than mine.

In fact, he could almost be Bobby's dad, especially since the two of them looked just alike, down to the thin black muscle shirt George was currently wearing and had obviously cut the sleeves off of long ago.

Maybe muscle shirts were a family trait. I briefly wondered if his dad and mom wore the same sort of clothes to their jobs.

"Bumper's junk," George said slowly, not taking his eyes off the car, "but there's no structural damage elsewhere."

"And that's a good thing," Bobby offered as a translation. He was instantly rewarded by Andy's smile.

"Well," George continued, "I know where we can get a bumper. And we can replace the headlight as well."

"Oh, thank God!" Andy proclaimed, clapping her hands in glee. "I am so, so happy to hear you say that. I don't care what it costs. I just have to get this fixed immediately."

"Andy!" I gasped, then dropped my voice to whisper. "You probably shouldn't say things like that."

Bobby, who had obviously overheard me from his position on the other side of Andy, shot me a hurt look and took Andy's hand. "George won't take advantage of her."

"Sorry," I said, a heated flush covering my face and throat. "I just saw a news report a few months ago that said girls were more likely to get ripped off by servicemen than guys were. I wasn't trying to insult your brother."

I chewed on my lower lip and forced myself to shut up. Maybe I should just stay quiet, eh? Creating bad blood with the guy who was going to fix Andy's car and thus save her from a lifelong grounding was not the best idea.

"Head inside," George said. "I'll pull the car out back to work on it. I'll call a buddy to help me get it done faster."

Andy nodded in relief, dropping the car key into his open hand. "Please take care of this," she said to him quietly.

We went inside Bobby's house, which was immaculately clean. And decorated to the T with feminine frills. Okayyyyy, definitely not what I was expecting to see in his house. I'd figured it would be wall-to-wall exercise equipment.

Bobby led us to the living room couch, which was covered in a deep-red rose pattern. "Would you two like something to drink?"

"Coke for me, please," Andy said, her butt perched on the edge of the couch.

"I'll have water," I answered, sitting beside her.

Bobby left.

Andy and I exchanged glances as we checked out the decor.

There were more doilies in here than I'd even known could possibly exist in one location. They were on the side tables, the coffee table . . . even draped over the arms of the couch—every piece of furniture was covered by at least two pristine white doilies.

It was like being in grandma hell. I briefly wondered if Grandma Cougar Mary's house looked like this.

"Bobby's mom crochets," Andy offered, grinning sheepishly. "She sells some of her stuff on the weekends at craft fairs." She dropped her voice and leaned toward me. "I've been here a few times, and it still surprises me."

"Yeah, you wouldn't think his house would be this . . ." I faltered, trying to find the right word.

"Girly?" Andy gave me a wry smile.

"Exactly. Hey, can I borrow your cell?" I asked. "Derek was out of school today, and I want to thank him for the mosaic."

She whipped it out of her pocket. "Have at it."

I slipped into the bathroom for some privacy, closed the door, and dialed his cell. It went right to voice mail. Crap.

"Um, it's Felicity. I noticed you weren't in school today. I hope you're not sick. Anyway, I wanted to . . ." I stalled. Actually, I didn't want to go into this in a voice mail. Especially while standing in

Bobby's bathroom. It just didn't feel right. "I wanted to talk to you. Can you give me a call at home tonight? Okay, I'll talk to you soon."

After I hung up, I went back into the living room and gave Andy her cell back. "Thanks so much."

Bobby returned, handing us our drinks in gold-rimmed glasses. "Here you go," he said, sitting on the other side of Andy. "Soooooo," he said, glancing at me, then Andy. "Can you believe the school year is almost over? I'll be glad for summer."

"Are you planning to work any?" I asked him.

He nodded. "My dad has me work at his landscaping company every summer. It's a good way to keep in shape." I saw him start to lift his arm to show his muscles, but he stopped, giving Andy a crooked grin and dropping his hand onto hers. "And to earn a little extra money so I can take Andy out, too."

She swatted him lightly. "Oh, come on. You know you don't need to do anything like that for me."

Wow, so Bobby was even getting over the self-bravado act and not feeling the need to flash his muscles to everyone around him. I never thought that would happen, but love does crazy things. Maybe Andy was a good influence on him and was helping him realize he didn't need to boast to make people like him.

He held his arm out, showing me a leather bracelet. "Check this out, Felicity. Andy bought this for me. Isn't it great?"

Andy blushed. "Come on now," she said, looking up into his eyes.

He leaned toward her.

"Well, I'm gonna go outside and watch them work on the car," I said, standing and stretching my arms over my head. A good cupid knows when to make a graceful exit and let a couple have time alone. "I'll be back in a little bit."

I slipped through the kitchen and through the back doors, settling into a seat on the patio. God, it felt good to be outside in actual warm sunshine. The winter had seemed to last for*ever*. I turned my face toward the sun and soaked up the rays for a couple of minutes.

I could hear George and his friend working on the car already. Well, that sounded promising.

Bobby's glee about the leather bracelet stuck in my head. It was a simple gift Andy had bought, but personal and from the heart. Maybe I could make something like that for Derek? That is, if we stayed together. God, I hope we weren't going to split up over all of this drama. I'd be so miserable without him. If he still wanted to be with me, I'd do my best to show him I cared about him. And if that meant making handicrafts and stuff like that, then I was willing to try.

Feeling a little better, I opened my eyes and glanced around. No one could see me. Maybe this was a good opportunity to matchmake some of those names on my list. It was time to end this cupid's block for good.

Whipping out my handy-dandy, ever-present LoveLine 3000, I pulled up some of the pending e-mails I'd created but had been too afraid to send. Janet had said I needed to build some kind of internal wall and distance myself when working. And boy, was she right. I knew instinctively that it was so much easier to matchmake couples if I didn't feel too personally vested in the results.

Drumming up all my courage, I sucked in a deep breath and forced myself to hit send on the love e-mail. There. The match was all done now . . . and if I'd made one match, surely I could make a few more.

I could totally do this.

After what felt like a thousand years but was in actuality only a couple of hours, the Porsche was finally finished. Fortunately, I'd managed to make six matches while we were waiting, including finding a person for Mrs. Kendel, so I was riding on a cupid high and feeling pretty damn good about it. If I could resolve this crap with Derek tonight, life would be completely perfect.

I'd only been sitting with Bobby and Andy again for a few minutes when George came into the living room.

"Whew," he said, wiping sweat off his rather large brow. A streak of dirt remained behind. "Okay, we're done."

Andy jumped off the couch. "Awesome. Let's go check it out!"

We ran out the back of the house toward the car, passing around the driver's side to check out the bumper. When I saw it, I swallowed hard and turned a quick eye toward Andy, hoping I was mistaken.

She stopped dead in her tracks, her eyes fixed on the front of the car. "That's not . . . how it's supposed to look."

Crap. I'd been right. I wasn't exactly a car expert or anything, but the color of the bumper he'd used wasn't even close to matching the original one. They were two different shades of red. Andy's dad would notice this for sure.

George's brow furrowed, and he said in a low voice, "I replaced the bumper and the headlight, as you requested."

"But the color of the bumper is completely wrong," she said, crossing her arms over her chest. "It isn't the same as what's on the car. My dad's going to know when he gets home. He's crazy about his car. He'll know it's been wrecked!"

"Maybe we're not looking at it right," Bobby said, two bright spots of color high on his cheeks. He stepped between George and Andy and tried to smile. "Let's just look closer." He leaned down and studied the two shades, not speaking for a long moment. He seemed to be trying to find something to help ease the tension, his mouth opening and closing several times in a row.

I came over to Andy's side. "Hey, the important thing is, he found a bumper that works. We can always go to the dealer and buy the paint. Or we could even ask if they'll paint it for us . . . don't they blend the color in with the rest of the car or something? And then your dad will never know."

That seemed to calm her a bit. "That could work," she said, turning her attention to me. "Let's go put this back under the tarp before my dad gets home."

"It'll be okay," Bobby said, his breath short and rapid. His eyes darted between Andy and George, as if he was unsure of where to place his loyalties.

Andy silently whipped out some cash from her back pocket

and handed it over to George. He dropped the key into her open palm, and she mumbled, "Thanks."

The ride back to Andy's house was pretty quiet. We rode in her dad's car, going almost ten miles under the speed limit the whole way. I think she was petrified to get in another accident . . . not that I could blame her.

I heard her suck in a shaky breath when we turned onto her street.

"God, I hope my mom is still out," she whispered. "Because all of this would be for nothing if she knew I had the car."

"It'll be okay," I said, feeling my own heart race with nervousness.

She pulled into the driveway and, using her dad's remote control, opened the garage door. It slid up easily, revealing an empty garage. Whew.

Andy navigated the Porsche in there and turned it off.

We hopped out quickly and threw the tarp back over the top, per our plan. As soon as possible, we would venture over to the dealer and see if we could find the paint we needed. But for now, in the dim garage light, the car looked just fine.

Andy patted down the back of the cover, then made her way

along the passenger's side and crossed in front of the car. "Thank God that's done. I—" At that moment she accidentally knocked her hip against the front of the car, causing the entire bumper to crash to the ground in a thunderous clang.

Standing in the garage doorway to the house, I froze, staring at the car in horror. I cupped my hand over my mouth. Dude, the bumper just fell off? What the hell did George use to affix it, a Band-Aid?

"Did that. Just. Happen?" Andy ground out through gritted teeth, staring at the bumper that peeked out of the bottom of the car cover.

My heart slammed in my chest. Poor Andy—she just couldn't get a break with this stupid car!

"Okay, okay, we can fix this," I said, rushing to her side. My hands gripped one side of the bumper. "Grab the other side. Maybe it just needs to be snugged in there a little tighter. Or maybe a bolt fell off or something." I had no idea what I was talking about, since I knew nothing about cars, but I tried to sound confident and strong for Andy's sake.

She flipped back the front of the tarp, then grabbed the other end. We heaved it back on the front, trying to see if it would fit in anywhere, but it just wouldn't stay on.

"OmigodwhatamIgoingtodoFelicity?" Her words came out in a breathless rush, and tears streaked down her cheeks.

It broke my heart to see her so upset. "Let's hide the bumper for now. We'll figure out an answer, I promise."

She lowered her bumper down, pushing it under the car against the front tires. I did the same. "I can't believe he didn't fix this right," she spat out, her eyes flaring in anger. "Now I'm stuck with a crappy bumper that doesn't even stay on!" Andy paused, and her voice got shaky. "Why would Bobby let him butcher the car like this?"

I covered the back of the car and took Andy's arm, leading her inside the house. "It's not Bobby's fault," I said gently. Yeah, I wasn't his biggest fan ever at the moment, but I could tell that Andy meant the world to him. "He'd be crushed if he knew this happened."

She sighed, plopping down onto her couch. "Yeah, you're right. I should have taken it to the dealer in the first place, I guess."

"Well, we'll definitely do that now. They can fix it, I bet."

They just had to, for poor Andy's sake.

Chapter 16

"So, where were you this morning?" I asked Derek in as calm a voice as I could muster, trying not to fiddle with my drawing pencil and give away my nervousness.

The spell Janet had cast over the two of us had worn off earlier today, Wednesday. Plus, our art class was the first I'd seen of him since our fight. He'd called me back last night at home, but my mom made me immediately get off the phone and do a pantload of laundry, so we didn't get a chance to say anything other than hi and bye.

Which, of course, had me massively paranoid that we didn't talk any today. Was Derek avoiding me? Was he trying to find a kind way to break up with me? Was I simply overreacting?

I just had to know, one way or the other.

"Sorry, I had to get the younger kids ready for school this morning," he said, his eyes still on his picture. "Mom asked me to help her out again because her feet are badly swollen."

Drawing in a deep breath, I stared at my drawing paper and whispered, "Look, I owe you some serious apologies. I'm truly sorry we got into that fight on Monday. I feel awful. And I feel even worse since I saw that gorgeous mosaic you made for me. It took my breath away."

I dared to glance up at his face. He was studying me quietly. His eyes weren't angry or cold, which I took to be a good sign. But he wasn't saying anything in response, so I continued to nervously babble.

"So anyway, I'm an ass, and I was totally rude when you were just trying to help me out. And—"

He reached a hand over and touched my arm. "I get too focused on trying to solve every problem. It wasn't right for me to take over when you just wanted some help." He paused, and his voice dropped down so quietly I could barely hear. "And I don't think I'm better than other people. Far from it."

His body was turned slightly toward me as we talked. During

my last TGIF sleepover, I'd read in *Cosmo* that this was definitely a plus. Maybe he still wanted to be with me.

"I know, and I'm sorry," I said again, trying to curb my increasing desire to cling to him and brashly ask if he was still into me.

Back off, I chided myself. I could scope him out without being a total spazz. Pushing him would just make things worse right now.

"So, how are your matches going?" he asked, tilting his paper to pencil in some darker shade lines around the edges of his still life drawing. "Did you finish them all?"

"Actually," I said, "I still have a few left to matchmake, but I think I got past my—"

"Shhhh," Mr. Bunch interrupted me, his eyes turning toward the two of us. "Quiet while you're working, please."

Whoops. I swallowed and nodded in assent.

Derek turned his attention back to his project. I tried to follow his lead. We worked in silence for a few more minutes. Not that I actually got any *work* done, of course. I was way too busy analyzing the situation in as professional a manner as I could.

Derek's thigh had just brushed against my leg ever so slightly. Somewhere, probably on *Oprah* or one of those kinds of shows, I'd heard that maintaining physical contact was important in relationships. So, signs like that could definitely be a positive.

Then again ... Derek's contact with me seemed more accidental than purposeful. Even if he could feel it and wasn't pulling away, he didn't seem to be trying to increase it.

And, even worse, he hadn't talked to me very much today. This worried me the most. When the cupid spell was still going on, he'd told me many times a day how often I was on his mind and how eager he was to see me.

But he hadn't told me this at all today. That could be the result of the spell wearing off. Or it could be residual issues from our fight. Or a combo of both.

My heart thudded painfully in my chest. What should I do? I fervently wished I could talk to someone about my problem.

I tried to imagine what advice Maya and Andy would give me. Maya would likely hug me and tell me I was overreacting. Andy would tell me that too but would then say I should try to remind Derek why he and I belonged together.

Good advice, Andy-in-my-brain! I could do that.

I perked up and leaned over toward Derek. "Are you looking forward to prom?"

He glanced up at me, his forehead creased. "Hey, about that—" he started but was cut off.

"Derek, Felicity, I'm not going to tell you again," Mr. Bunch said, openly glaring at us this time. "Zip it."

"Sorry," I mumbled. God, was he crabby or what? Who peed in his oatmeal this morning?

I turned my attention back toward my crappy drawing, but on the inside I was crumbling. What had Derek been about to tell me?

He nudged my leg with his knee, then tapped a finger on the corner of his picture. In faint letters, he'd written:

Let's talk after class

I nodded, trying to remain calm, rational, sensible. I could do this. I could focus on my art project until he and I could talk.

Well, I *told* myself that . . . but as I waited, it felt like time was traveling backward. I swear, it was almost painful to glance up at the clock and see the stupid minute hand not moving at all.

Every couple of minutes I glanced at Derek out of the corner of my eyes, silently hoping to find him looking at me. But when it had actually happened one time, the impact had nearly smacked me with shock, since I wasn't expecting it. I'd jerked my gaze away from his piercing eyes, suddenly embarrassed.

Finally someone took pity on me and ended my misery by ringing the school bell. Trying not to appear too anxious and thus turn Derek off, I forced myself to calmly put my stuff away and gather my belongings. We headed out of class and down the hall, going slowly to allow traffic to pass around us.

I started to reach my hand over to grasp his, at the same moment he shifted his backpack on his shoulder. I jerked my hand back, cramming it in the pocket of my jeans so I wouldn't look stupid.

A hot burn swept over my cheeks. Was it just bad timing, or was he avoiding any purposeful contact with me now? Things couldn't have gotten bad that quickly after the spell had worn off, could they?

Once we were alone and everyone else had cleared out of the hall, I coughed lightly, hoping the sound would prod him to speak. It worked.

"So," he said, casting me a sideways glance, "we were talking about prom before we were cut off."

Oh God, I felt like I was going to hurl due to my bundled nerves. This was just crazy overwhelming. I forced myself to nod.

"Anyway," he continued, "is it okay if we go to dinner early and then over to my parents' house? My mom wants to see us together."

That was it? Whew—okay, he wasn't dumping me as his date. I forced myself to take several calming breaths before I answered. "Oh, absolutely. Sure, that's no problem. I'd love to see your mom again. I really like her. She's so sweet."

I was babbling, and badly, but I couldn't stop gushing. I wanted him to see how enthusiastic I still was.

"Great."

An odd thought took hold of me as we headed down the hallway. What would he do if I confessed about the spell Janet put on us? It was over now, so surely she couldn't have any problem with me discussing it.

If I told him, would Derek assure me of his love? Or would it turn him off that he'd been matchmade against his will?

Would he be mad at me for keeping it a secret for this long?

No, there wasn't any reason for him to be pissed. It's not like I'd cast the spell myself. Maybe I should unburden this load off my shoulders. Then, if I could assume his feelings were still the same, he'd realize that we were meant to be together and would assure me of as much.

I licked my lips, trying to figure out the right way to broach the subject. "Hey, Derek."

"What?" he asked me.

"Ummmmm," I said, then chickened out. We were so tentative right now that this might push us over the edge and break us up for good. And I just couldn't risk it. "Nothing. Never mind."

Derek sighed, frowning a little. I knew he could tell I was still keeping things inside, but he didn't say anything about it. He glanced at his watch. "I gotta go. I have to watch my brothers and sisters while Mom goes to her doctor's appointment this afternoon."

Disappointment gripped my gut. I shrugged nonchalantly, though, not wanting to show how I felt. Words babbled out of my mouth. "That's fine with me, since I have homework and stuff, anyway. You know, the House Nazi always has some new chore for me to do, like scrubbing stuff that no one wants to touch. Maybe you can call me later—if you get time, I mean. If you want."

He nodded.

Impulsively, I leaned forward onto my tiptoes and kissed him on the lips, relishing the sensation. "Maybe we can go out again soon. I'll give you a call later."

"Yeah, that should work." He smiled, said good-bye, then

turned down the hallway, his steady gait moving him away from me.

I closed my eyes and pinched the bridge of my nose with my thumb and forefinger, sighing heavily. As much as people liked to claim that girls were hard to read, I think I could prove that guys were even harder.

TGIF, and we were at Maya's house this time for our sleepover, since she wanted to stick close to her mom. I couldn't blame her— poor Mrs. Takahashi was like a zombie, wandering room to room with a dust rag and polishing furniture she'd already cleaned several times since I'd been there.

It was heartbreaking . . . and even more so because I understood her pain, her attempts to feel some sort of normalcy in her life even though everything was upside down.

No, Derek hadn't dumped me . . . yet. But with every day that passed, I could almost feel the ax coming down. Not that he was overtly doing anything cruel, but every gesture he made toward me felt like it had lessened in romantic intensity. Things were definitely different.

The best I could do was to try to act like nothing was wrong, to try to keep on moving forward and continue appearing confident and steady.

"I feel like seeing a movie night," Maya proclaimed, plopping her pajama-bottomed self down in front of the DVD shelf. "What should we watch? We can take it up to my room."

Andy, who'd just gotten back downstairs after changing into her nightclothes, shrugged. "Whatever you want. Just nothing with cars in it." She grimaced.

"Did you get a chance to call the dealership yesterday or today?" I asked her in a quiet voice. Not that I thought Mrs. Takahashi would call Andy's folks and rat her out, but one couldn't be too careful.

"I called them last night, but they told me I'd have to bring it in for them to examine." She rubbed the back of her neck, then pulled her hair into a loose ponytail, using the holder from around her wrist.

"Well, let's do that tomorrow," I suggested. I straightened the leg of my favorite pair of old flannel jammies that had gotten twisted somehow.

"Can't. Dad's gonna be home." Her voice took a shaky edge. "He's going to discover what happened, I just know it."

Poor Andy. We'd managed to sneak back into the garage and hold the bumper against the car with some bungee cables (which gave the illusion that the car was fine—a brilliant idea I'd had, thank you very much), but it was obviously only a temporary fix.

"How about you treat your parents to a special lunch—and while they're out, you can get the car fixed?" Maya suggested. "That way they can't refuse the invitation, especially if you've already made all the arrangements and reserved a table for them."

"That might work. This is getting *so* expensive, though." She dropped down beside Maya, releasing a big puff of air through her pinched lips.

"Hey, I like Maya's idea . . . what if you give them a Burger Butler gift card the next time you're at work? I'm sure they'd love that," I teased Andy.

She shot me a mock glare, wrinkling her face. "Oh yeah, that's a fabulous idea. We all know that's the gift that keeps on giving."

Maya and Andy picked a movie starring some new hottie actor, and we headed upstairs to watch it on Maya's big computer screen. The two of them squeezed in on her bed together, propping their backs up with pillows and draping a light blanket over their legs. I sat on the floor right in front of them, leaning back against the bed.

"Maybe this'll cheer me up," Andy said, rubbing her hands in anticipation. "The lead guy's supposed to be really good. And even better, he doesn't wear a shirt for, like, half the movie."

I groaned, giggling. "I should have known that's what appealed to you."

My stomach growled. Whoops. I never was one who could watch a movie without having something to chow on. Guess I had my body trained to expect food. I glanced over at the bowl of chocolate-covered pretzels beside me that was totally empty.

Maya faced me, eyes wide. "Holy crap, was that you?"

"Go get some food, girl," Andy said, one eyebrow raised. "You sound like you haven't eaten in a week."

"Hey, shut up, guys!" I shot back, crossing my arms like I was mad, for dramatic effect. "Just for that, I'm going to get ice cream and totally not share with either of you."

I headed downstairs toward the kitchen, where I grabbed a small pint of delicious rocky road ice cream and a spoon. I could almost taste the sweetness in my mouth and forced myself not to drool on the carton.

As I passed back through the first floor and toward the stairs, I noticed Mrs. Takahashi sitting on the couch, the dust rag draped across her sweatpants. Crap, she must have dug her sweats out of the back of her car before Maya could pitch them.

Following my impulse, I headed over to the sofa and sat beside her.

There was a sad silence between us for a long moment. Then she sniffled and said, "I'm okay, really. You can go upstairs with the girls, but thank you." She propped her small, sock-clad feet on the coffee table.

"I know I'm not a grown-up, but I know how it feels to be disappointed in love," I started, thinking about Derek. "And how you feel worried that your heart is completely out of your hands and in the grasp of someone who has the power to make you hurt."

She swallowed, nodding seriously in response. "Yeah, love isn't always what you think it's going to be."

That's one thing I really liked about Maya's mom—she didn't try to shoo me off or tell me to butt out of adult business, like some parents did. Yeah, I wasn't technically an adult yet, but I was close . . . and I'd seen and experienced more than my share of adult feelings.

I handed her the spoon and ice cream. "I think you need this even more than I do."

She took them, giving me a small smile of thanks. "Maybe we can share."

"Good idea." I ran back to grab a spoon from the kitchen, then sat beside her and propped my feet on the coffee table. We took turns eating delicious bites.

"Thank you for being such a good friend to Maya," Mrs. Takahashi said. "She's going to need you and Andy over the next few months—" She stopped, her voice sounding like her throat had closed up. After clearing her throat and sucking back a few sobs, she continued, "Because it's going to be a rough ride."

A rough ride. I'd heard someone say those words before. . . . Oh, wait. Maya had gotten her fortune told by Absinthia, a Goth girl at our school. She'd warned Maya that the next few months were going to be hard. "A rough ride," I think were her exact words.

She'd been spot-on in her tarot-card reading. Maybe I could scrounge up the courage and the cash to see if Absinthia would do a reading for me, too. She might have an interesting perspective about Derek that I hadn't considered . . . or at least give me a heads-up on when the axe would fall.

I sighed, sinking further back into the couch and digging into another bite of ice cream. A couple of drops slid off my spoon and onto my pants. "Crap," I mumbled, wiping the mess off my leg. Great—that was totally going to stain. How very attractive.

Oh, well. What was the point of trying to look attractive,

anyway? It hadn't made Derek love me more. He hadn't responded at all to my makeover attempt. Maybe Mrs. Takahashi had the right idea, not caring about her looks and wearing whatever made her feel comfy.

I glanced over at her. Was this going to be me in twenty years—sitting on my couch, spilling food on my clothes and not caring? Or even sooner, should he and I break up?

The thought depressed me, and I blinked back tears. Maybe one can't change fate, regardless of what efforts are made. Mrs. Takahashi had worked her ass off trying to lure her husband back, to no avail.

"Felicity!" Andy yelled from upstairs. "Did you fall in a hole? You're missing all the shirtless scenes!"

"Go on back upstairs," Maya's mom said with a halfhearted smile, waving me away. "I'm fine, thanks. Just keep Maya happy tonight, okay?"

I hugged her quickly, then I went back to Maya's room, gently closing the door behind me.

"Sorry, guys," I said. "I got sidetracked talking to Maya's mom."

"How's she doing?" Maya asked, standing. "I should go down and check on her."

"It's okay," I said, tugging on her sleeve. "Your mom sent me up here and told me she's fine."

Which was a bald-faced lie. I knew she wasn't fine. Maya's mom knew it too. But for now, I'd respect her wish and help Maya have a good evening . . . even if I wasn't feeling too happy myself.

Chapter 17

"Any calls for me?" I asked Mom when I got home on Saturday morning, bleary-eyed and half asleep on my feet. Maya, Andy, and I had sat up half the night yapping and watching movies, so I'd gotten almost no rest, a strategy I hadn't started regretting until I'd had to rouse my sorry self out of bed and head home this morning.

Boy, was I feeling it now. Blech.

Mom shook her head, moving toward the kitchen. "Nope. No calls."

I shrugged, trying to ignore the disappointed sting in my stomach, and followed her into the kitchen. "That's fine, thanks."

"Well, Derek knows you go to your sleepovers on Friday,"

Mom offered. She picked up the dish towel and slung it over her forearm. "I'm sure he'll call you today."

Was I that transparent? Or was she just that astute?

I blushed, suddenly embarrassed. "Things have just changed recently between us. You know how guys are, I'm sure."

She walked over to me, concern etched on her face. "You look tired," she said, sweeping the hair out of my eyes. "You should go back upstairs and get some more sleep. I'm sure that will help you feel better."

I nodded, glancing at my watch. Maybe she was right. Some rest would clear my mind and help me see things in a new light, and I could still get up in time to go with Andy to the car dealership this afternoon while her parents were at lunch.

"Okay." I gave Mom a quick hug and darted upstairs. Time to heed the siren call of my warm, awaiting bed.

As soon as my head hit the pillow, I conked out, not waking for two solid hours until my bedside phone rang.

"Hello?" I asked in a sleep-grogged voice, trying to clear the sleep from my eyes. Was it time for me to meet Andy already?

Though I squinted hard, I couldn't see the time on my alarm clock through my blurry eyes.

"Hey," Derek said, his low, familiar tone surprising me.

Instantly, I sat up in my bed, my pulse surging. "Oh, Derek. Hey!" I said, trying to sound perky and not like I was half-dead.

He cleared his throat. "I know this is last minute, but do you wanna grab a burger or something for lunch?"

Aw, crap! A golden opportunity, and I couldn't take it.

I slapped my forehead. "I would, if I hadn't already promised Andy I'd meet her. She . . . needs to get her car fixed," I said vaguely, figuring Andy wouldn't want me to embarrass her and tell the circumstances behind our visit. "Can we go out Sunday, though?"

"Sure, that'll work. Guess I'd better give you more notice," Derek replied, his voice light. "I had no idea you were so popular."

Me? Was he joking? Because we both knew that in our relationship, I was *so* not the popular one.

"*You're* friends with everyone in school, not me." I could feel the tension, the edge of jealousy, seeping into my voice, so I tried to relax. There was no way I wanted to get into another fight with him. "Though I bet the love spell I accidentally set on you probably had a small hand in it. Maybe some of the students are still madly in love with you."

He chuckled. "I sure hope not. I'm still trying to scrub the 'I heart Derek' graffiti off my mom's car."

There was a knock on my door.

"Felicity," my mom said, briefly poking her head in. "Andy's downstairs waiting for you."

"Okay, thanks," I answered Mom. "I gotta go," I told Derek, regret spilling into my voice. God, how badly I wanted to just run up and hug him tightly. I needed to feel his arms around me right now. But I couldn't tell him that without sounding desperate and clingy. Trying to keep my voice even, I continued, "I'll call you later, though, okay?"

I heard some mumbled talking in the background, which Derek responded to, his hand cupped over the phone. "Sure," he finally said to me. "Bye."

I placed the phone in the cradle and sat for a moment with my hand on the phone, mentally replaying the conversation. A sensation of paranoia swept over me. Derek wasn't usually one to ask me out on such short notice. And he'd seemed really distracted at the end of our conversation.

What did he want to talk to me about? He hadn't decided to end our relationship already, had he?

I toyed with the idea of not calling him back. Maybe if I stuck my head in the sand like a good little ostrich, all of this badness would go away.

Well, that's just dumb, I told myself, shaking my head in disgust. Better to man up—er, so to speak—and face this mess head-on. If Derek was going to break up with me, I was better off preparing myself for it instead of wishing it away.

Not that the idea didn't make me want to hurl all over the place.

Footsteps ran up my stairs and my door flew open, revealing Andy, who was twirling the key ring on her index finger.

"Hey, you ready to go? The bumper looks like it's going to fall off any minute," she said, then paused, tilting her head to the side. "What's with the weird look on your face? Are you sick?"

"No, I'm fine," I said brightly, pasting on a huge, fake smile. This wasn't the time to whine about my problems. Right now I needed to be a good friend to Andy and help her resolve the car issue.

At least that was something under our control.

"But is the owner of the car here?" Juan, the thin guy behind the counter, asked with one raised eyebrow, leaning forward to look over our shoulders.

Closing her eyes, Andy drew in a slow, deep breath. I could see a vein throbbing on the side of her forehead. Not that I could blame her. We'd been standing in line for twenty minutes to talk to the repairman at the dealership. And now that we'd finally gotten to the front of the line, he wouldn't listen to us at all.

"Look," Andy said through pinched lips. I could tell she was trying to keep her tone even so she wouldn't rip this guy a new butthole. Getting on his bad side wasn't going to help the problem. "I just told you, I'm helping out my parents by fixing the car for them. I have money, I promise, and will be more than happy to pay for the repairs in advance."

Juan shook his head. "Sorry, but we can't work with anyone but the owners of the vehicle. Since you're a minor, and not listed as an owner, there's nothing we can do to help you."

Andy turned and looked at me, frustration knitting her eyebrows together. I could practically see steam coming out of her ears.

"Give us just one second, please," I said to Juan, then pulled Andy to the side. "Okay, what now?"

Tears welled in her eyes, and she shrugged. "I'm screwed. No way will I be able to convince them to fix it. My dad will kill me when he finds out."

A lump clogged my throat. "I'm sorry. If you want, I'll come with you when you talk to him. Maybe he'll go easier on you if I'm there."

She sniffled.

I hugged her tightly, wishing I could take this bad situation away. She had to be dreading the inevitable.

I'd only seen her dad pissed off once before. When Andy and I were in fifth grade, we'd decided to play beauty shop and use his hair clippers to cut our Cabbage Patch Kids' hair. Yeah, not the brightest idea. He made us do chores around their house for two weeks to make up the cost of buying a new hair clipper.

Andy chuckled, as if knowing exactly what I was thinking. "I appreciate your offer," she said, mumbling into my shoulder, "but I think I'd better just face him on my own. He might not like me using you as a shield."

I nodded slowly. If only there were another way, but everything seemed to be conspiring against us.

We left the car repair shop in the Porsche and headed back to Andy's house, making sure to travel slowly and carefully. When we arrived, I gave her another huge hug, wished her good luck, and then headed back to my house.

Once there, I went up to my room and logged on to my computer to check e-mail. Nothing new but spam, of course. Then I loaded up my blog and created a new private entry.

I can't believe how chaotic everything is!

Poor Andy's going to be in deep, deep trouble when her dad finds out about his car. I hope he still lets her go to prom, because we've been planning this, like, forever. It doesn't seem fair to ground her from the only junior prom she'll ever get to go to, especially since she's willing to pay to fix the car.

And if she does get to go, I hope she doesn't get mad at Bobby because his brother is a terrible mechanic.

In just as horrible news, Maya's mom seems to have totally given up on true love. What a terrible place to be, to lose hope like that. She looked so bad when I saw her, so empty. Like a shell of who she used to be.

All I can do is hold on to my own inner strength . . . if there's even any left in me at this point.

I saved and closed the entry, then turned off my PC and worked on homework for a bit, staying near the phone to wait for

Andy's call. She was going to let me know what happened after all was said and done.

A full hour passed. I itched to call her, even picking up the phone twice and starting to dial her number, but it was probably a bad idea to interrupt whatever was going on.

Finally the phone rang. I jumped up and grabbed it.

"Hello?" I answered anxiously.

"Hey," Andy whispered into the mouthpiece, her voice thick and heavy like she'd been crying.

"Oh no," I breathed, heart thudding in my chest. "You sound awful. What happened? Are you okay?"

"Yeah, I'm fine. It was just very hard. I'm hiding in my bathroom right now, but I wanted to call you so you wouldn't worry. Dad was furious, but he appreciated my honesty with him. I'm grounded for three months, and I'm not allowed to drive." She paused. "Since I'm paying him back for the repair costs, he's going to let me go to prom."

"No way!" I squealed. "That's not too bad at all, Andy."

"No kidding. He's going to drop me off at prom and pick me back up at nine thirty. Which is superlame, but at least I get to go," she said. I heard some rustling. "Gotta go. We'll talk on Monday."

We hung up.

I pushed my homework to the foot of my bed and lay back, crossing my hands behind my head. Andy had faced the challenge head-on and had come out of it with some punishment, but not nearly as bad as we'd feared. For that, I was thrilled for her.

And so, so proud.

"So, I have something for you," I told Derek Sunday evening in my living room. He could only stop by for a few minutes since it was late, so I needed to get right to the point.

"Really?" Derek shifted on the couch, leaning back and giving me a curious look. His knees brushed against mine.

I swallowed, then dug into my pocket. I'd spent most of yesterday evening working on this project for Derek, inspired by Andy's gift to Bobby. But instead of just buying Derek something, I'd decided to make it.

Which, in retrospect, was not my best idea. It had taken me three attempts to get the necklace looking halfway decent. It still wasn't perfect, but if I'd kept going at it, it would never be done. And it was important to me to give it to him today.

I pressed the folded leather necklace into his hand. "Here. I made it. But if you don't like it, I won't be offended or anything, I promise." Geez, why was I so nervous? It wasn't nearly as impressive as his mosaic. It wasn't even in the same galaxy.

He stretched it out to its full length, and I saw all the lumpy flaws in it where my fingers weren't able to weave the leather tightly enough. I had to fight the urge to rip it back out of his fingertips. He'd probably think it was stupid or—

"I love it." He tied it around his neck, then leaned over and pressed a soft kiss against my lips. I saw him swallow. "No one's ever made me a gift before."

"It was no biggie, really." But his words made me feel better. Even if I wasn't as skilled at artistic endeavors as he was, at least he seemed truly appreciative. "I know it can't compare, but it's just a small thank-you for the mosaic you made of me." I paused, clearing my throat. "Um, speaking of, do you think it would be okay if I got to . . . have the portrait after the art show is over?"

"You want it?" he asked, his brows knitted. "Really?"

I blinked. "Are you on crack? It's amazing. I'd be honored."

He smiled softly, his finger brushing the leather of his necklace. "Then it's yours."

"Thank you." I knew I'd treasure the portrait he'd done of me always, regardless of what happened between us in the future. But at least right now, in this moment, we were sharing with each other and feeling happy.

And this was something I'd never forget.

Geez, was she *ever* going to get here?

On Wednesday night, I glanced at my watch for the thousandth time since I'd arrived at Pizza Hut, waiting for Rob's girlfriend, Annette, to show up. It didn't help that I was starving to death, too, and ready to order a massively large pizza. And the Coke I was chugging wasn't filling my stomach at all.

With all the drama going on in my life lately (hah, like *that* was anything new), I'd completely forgotten about doing the rest of my "interview" with Annette about being a female cop. Luckily, she'd asked me about it at Sunday dinner—and of course, since my whole family was there and staring expectantly at me, I couldn't back out of it.

So we'd agreed to meet, nosh on some pizza (my treat, since she was generously donating her time), and finish up our discussion.

However, it was now . . . seven fifteen, according to my watch. And she was supposed to have been here at seven.

I crossed my arms, sighing heavily.

Don't be so uptight, I ordered myself. After all, Annette was a cop. Maybe there was some kind of emergency that delayed her, like a bad accident on the highway. Those kinds of things should be her priority.

I suddenly felt bad about being so irritated. Not very grateful of me, especially since she didn't have to meet me at all.

Geez, what was happening to my attitude lately? Everything was sending me into extremes. This was getting out of control.

There was only one thing I could do.

I made a solemn, silent vow to myself, right there on the cracked red booth seat of Pizza Hut. I was going to show more tolerance, caring, and patience with the people around me. Time and time again, I'd seen how life's unexpected moments, no matter how big or small, could affect someone's life.

And it was my job as a decent human being to respond in the most understanding way I could.

Outside the window I saw a squad car pull into a nearby parking spot. Finally, Annette was here. And what fortuitous timing.

See? I felt a smile break out on my face. This new positive attitude was already bringing results.

Even though I knew it was a fake interview, I was looking forward to talking to her. This was a great opportunity for me to find out how her relationship with Rob was going, and from her point of view. I could easily tell how my brother had been affected, but I wanted to hear how happy she was too.

Annette, in the passenger's seat, talked animatedly to her partner, who was driving the car. Oh crap, the driver was Officer Banks, the guy who'd busted me outside the bar when I had spied on Rob.

I crossed my fingers and hoped he wasn't coming in, because I was soooo not wanting to deal with—

Right then Annette leaned over toward the officer and gave him a kiss on his mouth.

Chapter 18

At first, a large part of my brain didn't seem to comprehend what was going on. It even tried to excuse the scene I'd just witnessed, but the other part of my brain knocked the excuse out like a prize fighter on steroids:

Delusional side of brain: Maybe Annette's just being friendly, and that's how she tells her partner good-bye. They could be good buddies.

Rational side of brain: Who tells a friend good-bye by sticking your tongue in their mouth? I've never told any of my friends good-bye like that, and for good reason . . . because that's called making out!

No, I knew exactly what had happened here. Annette had lost the flame she'd once carried for my brother. The cupid spell had apparently worn off. Which utterly sucked, because I knew beyond a shadow of a doubt that Rob was still madly in love with her.

In fact, I had talked to him not more than an hour ago to let him know my meeting with his girlfriend was still on, and he'd gushed about what a great time I was going to have with her. Poor Rob.

My stomach clenched in a tighter knot, and I fought another wave of sickness sweeping over me. I'd seen some crazy behavior from people I'd matchmade, but I'd never seen a person so brazenly make out with someone else on the day the spell had worn off. I doubted Annette had even had time to break up with Rob beforehand.

Annette finished licking the inside of Officer Banks's mouth and backed her way out of the car. She waggled her fingers good-bye to him, closing the door and strolling up the sidewalk. Toward me.

I couldn't do this. No way was I going to be able to get through dinner with her. My brain whirred, considering my options:

1—hide in the bathroom or under the table, where she can't see me

2—confront her about what I saw and risk her wrath

3—fake an illness and barf all over her

Well, it was too late for number one. The bathroom stood to the side of the front door, and she was coming inside now, walking toward me with her typical friendly smile. Her big, fat, lying smile.

"Felicity," Annette greeted me warmly. She slid into the booth across from me, and I heard her holster scrape against the back of the booth bench. "Sorry I'm late. Thanks for being so understanding, though."

Option two, or three? Two, or three?

I opened my mouth and let fly the first words that came out. "That's okay. Actually, I'm gonna have to bail. I feel like I'm going to be sick." With a dramatic groan, I clutched my stomach.

It was the truth. My stomach was churning like there was a tub of boiling butter inside it. Somehow, confronting Annette about what I'd seen seemed a lot less appealing when I was feeling icky. Plus, she had a gun on her. Not that I thought she'd shoot me or anything, but it was still intimidating.

She frowned, her back straightening. "Well, I'm sorry to hear that. Maybe we can finish your interview some other time."

Briefly, I wondered if she knew that *I* knew, or if she had grown suspicious. But given that she'd kissed Officer Banks so boldly, and right there in the parking lot, I highly doubted she cared about my opinion. She obviously didn't care what Rob thought, either, and he was supposedly her boyfriend.

I fought back the sneer that was trying to edge its way onto my face and rose from the booth, dropping a twenty-dollar bill on the table. "Here, please order yourself some dinner. After all, you did come all this way to talk to me." Then I turned and fled.

The whole ride home, I debated with myself about whether or not I should tell Rob about what I'd seen. Was it my place to tell him his girlfriend was playing kissy face with another officer? Part of me screamed that yes, if I were him, I'd want to know.

The other part reminded me of the cliché "don't shoot the messenger." There was a reason it was good to not butt into someone's love life in this way—because, inevitably, you ended up getting blamed yourself. And maybe this was something Rob needed to figure out for himself.

I pulled into the driveway, turned off the car, and trudged

through the front door. Mom and Dad were in the living room, watching TV.

"Hey," Dad said, glancing up with a smile.

I nodded in response. Wordlessly I handed Mom the car keys and made my way upstairs, draping across my bed with my head over the side, staring at the floor. A minute passed, and then there was a light knock on my door.

"Felicity, are you okay?" Mom asked through the thin plywood. "Can I come in and talk to you?"

"Sure," I mumbled, edging my body over on the mattress as she sat beside me.

"What's going on?"

"I have a bit of a conflict," I said, filled with a sudden urge to confide in someone. Mom often had good advice—when I asked for it, at least—and maybe she could help shed some light on what I should do. "I . . . saw something that's really going to hurt someone else. And I don't know if I should tell that person or not."

She sighed, rubbing my back. "That's a tough call. Sometimes people don't like it when you butt into their business. But there's something to be said for being honest. What do you think is the right thing to do?"

I leaned my face to the side, pressing my right cheek against my warmed bedspread. "I don't know. I guess I should tell."

We were silent for a moment.

Then she gently cleared her throat. "Sometimes, the right thing isn't always the easy thing."

Mom was right. I mean, look at Andy. It took massive courage to admit to her dad what had happened with his Porsche. And she knew for sure her confession was going to have a negative repercussion, but she still did it, anyway.

At least Rob would know I was telling him because I cared.

I sat up and hugged Mom. Yeah, she was a bit of a House Nazi, but she was still pretty darn smart. "Thanks. You're right."

She chuckled. "I have my moments."

"I should make a call," I said, picking up my phone. It was time to put on my big girl panties and deal.

"I'll leave you alone." She patted my back one last time and left the room.

Big girl panties or no, my hands were shaky as I dialed Rob's cell phone.

"Mom?" he said after picking the phone up.

"No, it's me, Felicity." I struggled to keep my voice calm and normal.

"Oh, hey. How did your meeting with Annette go?"

God, he sounded so full of hope and happiness, even just saying her name. And here I was, the brutal romance killer who was going to crush his heart by revealing the infidelities of his true love.

"I . . . left early," I said.

"Oh. How come? Don't you need to finish your interview?"

"Rob, I saw something I probably shouldn't have," I blurted out.

"Did you file a report?" he asked, instantly turning on his cop voice. "Was it some sort of crime?

Only a crime against the heart. "No, it wasn't that kind of thing. It was . . . well . . ." Now that the moment was here, I wasn't sure how to say it.

I heard Rob's walkie-talkie go off, and a deep male voice spoke rapidly.

"Gotta go, Felicity. Police emergency. Can we talk later?"

"Sure," I whispered, closing my eyes.

Chicken! I could have told him by now if I hadn't stalled. Maybe there was time to say something, though, so he'd at least keep his eyes open.

"Rob," I continued, "just . . . be careful, okay? I'd hate to see you get hurt."

"Okayyy," he drawled. "Later."

Yes, later. I'd take some time to plan out my approach so I wouldn't be so tongue-tied the next time we talked. And there *would* be a next time.

Thursday, during lunch, I made up some lame excuse and sneaked away from Maya and Andy. There was no way in hell I wanted them to know I was going to consult Absinthia, resident super Goth, to get my fortune told. I remembered how much Andy had mocked Maya's reading. Even though I'd been skeptical myself, I couldn't deny Absinthia had been dead-on in her predictions.

I wound my way outside school and toward the steady streams of smoke pouring up from underneath the slats of the track field bleachers, her usual hangout.

"—you're crazy," one of the guys in her group was saying. He puffed on his cigarette, exhaling the smoke in an O shape from his mouth. "Hunter S. Thompson knew the effect he was having on his news reports, but he still chose to put himself right in the story."

"No kidding," Absinthia said, nodding in agreement. "He was a genius."

"Um, excuse me," I said, standing off to the edge behind them. "Can I talk to you, Absinthia?"

She turned to face me, pressing the stubby, ashy end of her cigarette on the ground. "So, you're back," she said, one eyebrow raised high. "What brings you out here? Does your friend need another reading?"

I cleared my throat. "Actually, *I'd* like one."

A dozen black-lined eyes fixed on me in disbelief. Obviously they'd remembered Andy's and my skepticism.

My cheeks flushed with embarrassment. Geez, I could see this was a dumb idea.

"But you're busy," I continued in a rapid speech, wishing I hadn't come out here in the first place. "See ya later."

"I'll do it," Absinthia said, standing.

Whew. I swallowed my relieved sigh, trying to keep cool.

"Let's go over to the other side of the bleachers. Do you have money?"

"Yup." I took the folded bill out of my pocket, handed it over, and followed her. We headed along the underside of the bleachers to where there was a flat concrete surface.

Absinthia sat down on it and crossed her legs, pulling the

cards, wrapped in velvety red fabric, out of her pants pocket. "Okay, I'm going to do a three-card reading of the major arcana. Have a seat." She pulled out the cards in question, shuffled them, then stretched out the red fabric and laid the stack of cards facedown on the cloth.

I did as she'd requested, my heart thudding painfully in anticipation as I watched her ring-covered fingers.

"Split the deck."

My hand shook as I reached over and divided the cards in two. She put them back together in reverse order, then fanned them out on the cloth. "Draw three cards. One will be your past, one your present, and one your future."

I studied the backs of the tarot cards, seeing if my intuition would tell me which ones I should choose. But nothing in me spoke up, so I simply picked three random ones and handed them to her.

Absinthia flipped the first one over in one deft turn. The Death card.

Crap. *Not* a good way to start this. My stomach lurched.

She smiled patiently, probably used to her clients freaking out whenever they got a horrible card. "Relax. This doesn't mean 'death,' per se."

Oh, that's right. I vaguely remembered her mentioning that when she did Maya's reading. I drew in a slow breath and forced myself to relax, shifting my legs. "So what does it mean, then?"

"You experienced an important change in your recent past, within the last few months. Something that upheaved your life drastically. It also caused unexpected pain as you felt the repercussions of that change."

She had to be talking about my cupid job, which for sure was a huge change . . . with its share of challenges. And pain. So many matches I'd made hadn't worked out. So many broken hearts.

I nodded. "Yeah, that makes sense."

"I sense you tried to force some actions in response to this big change, which didn't work." She raised that one eyebrow at me again, a small grin on her face. "Bit of a control freak, aren't you?"

Boy, two minutes into the reading and she already had me pegged.

"I guess so," I said noncommittally, not wanting to reveal all my weaknesses.

"Okay, this next card describes your present situation." She flipped over the next card. The Hanged Man.

Could the image staring up at me look any more miserable? Gee, this reading was making me feel *so* much better.

She clucked her tongue. "Things are a little . . . unbalanced for you right now, are they? Like the rug's been swept out from under you. I sense there's chaos in everything you touch . . . sometimes turning out for the good, but sometimes not."

"Very much so," I said, unable to prevent the emotional hitch in my voice. "But what can I do about it? How can I make things right? I've messed up a lot of stuff, and I don't know how to fix anything anymore."

Like how to make Maya's mom happy. Or how to make Derek love me without a spell influencing him. And the list went on and on.

She shook her head. "I think you're going about this the wrong way. Until you learn how to go with the flow, until you acknowledge and control your pride, nothing's going to get better for you."

Pride? Was it so wrong to have a sense of duty and satisfaction from making a good match or helping people? And wasn't that what Janet had hired me for?

"I don't see how I've done so badly here," I said stiffly. "I'm doing exactly what I'm supposed to."

"Hey, I'm just the messenger," she said with a casual shrug, raising her palms up toward me.

The messenger. She was right. How easy it was to get angry with the person just trying to help.

With a guilty twinge, I remembered how I'd hoped my brother would take the news of Annette when I finally got a chance to tell him. Not angry and resentful, like I was at the moment, but with an open heart and mind.

"Sorry," I whispered. "I'm a little sensitive about this topic."

"I can tell." She paused. "I sense there's someone else involved here, too . . . someone you're pushing too hard. You need to relax and trust in others. Let them handle things, too. For you, that may be the greatest sacrifice you can make. But once you do, you'll finally be righted on to your feet again."

Surely she was talking about Derek. Was she right—was I really forcing things with him? But if I didn't work hard, how was anything going to happen between us? After all, things slipped out of my hands and went down the crapper when I didn't fight to make the situation right. And even though he and I had some great, memorable moments together, they were becoming fewer and further between.

Eventually they'd just fade away altogether.

I was already seeing evidence of this happening. Derek didn't even try to find me in the mornings anymore. In fact, the only time I really saw him in school now was in art class. For the eight-billionth time, I rued the fact that I didn't even have a cell phone. We couldn't send texts to check in with each other, like most normal couples did.

I gave a begrudging shrug, not willing to believe what she was saying. "I guess."

"And now, your last card that shows the future." She flipped over The Sun. "This isn't a bad one at all."

I sighed in relief. It was about time. The whole reading so far hadn't been as gentle as I'd expected, or hoped. "So what does it mean?"

"The Sun means there's going to be a time of positive well-being in your future." She stopped and stared hard at me. "But those times will only come about so long as you are careful to adapt and remain flexible and not let your pride overrule you. Some pride is a good thing, but too much can make a person rigid and arrogant."

Okay, I was totally sensing a theme here, and I didn't like it. How many more times was she going to tell me what a bad person I was?

I stood. "Well, thank you very much for your time," I forced myself to say politely.

Absinthia wrapped up her cards and grabbed a pack of cigarettes out of her pocket, pulling out one and lighting it. Her face was neutral, but her eyes studied me with interest. "I don't normally tell clients this, but I can sense you're a very powerful person with the capacity to do great things. The cards you drew were strong, emotional ones."

I swallowed, staring at her silently.

She popped the cigarette in her mouth and drew in a big puff, then stood up and headed under the bleachers, turning to look at me. She gave me a small smile. "Once you learn balance and figure out how to get past this rough patch of your life, you'll be good to go."

Shame surged through me. She was obviously trying to leave me with a positive note, and I was being ungrateful. I didn't know what to make of her reading, but it didn't mean she was insincere in her efforts. Nor was she trying to force anything on me—she was simply reading what she'd seen in the cards.

"Thank you," I said humbly.

"Any time," she replied, then walked off to rejoin her group.

I made my way back into school, heading through the double doors right as the bell rang. Absinthia had said some stuff that stung, and other stuff that had to be flat-out wrong, but maybe within her message there was a grain of truth.

Now to figure it out.

Chapter 19

Prom night had finally arrived, and I was a bundle of raw, excited nerves. I stood in front of my mirror and fiddled with my hair for the thousandth time. What would Derek think of my dress?

Of me?

I'd had so little time to talk to him over the past couple of days, and our only real correspondence was through e-mail, where he'd sent me a brief message about how swamped he was now that his mom was getting closer to giving birth. I wish he'd picked up the phone to call me instead, but I tried to push my insecurity aside and focus on here and now.

The only positive aspect about having so much time to myself this week was that I'd finished all but a small handful of my matches. Tonight would be the conclusion for our competition—though I had a strong gut feeling that Derek's lasting matches would greatly outnumber mine.

"Felicity, he's here," I heard my mom say from downstairs.

"I'm coming," I replied. With shaky hands, I smoothed my dress and headed downstairs to face my destiny.

Derek was standing in the living room, his face turned toward the staircase as I descended. His black tux fit him well, and the black vest hugged his torso nicely.

He smiled, bright teeth gleaming, and his eyes raked over me. My lips tingled under his appreciative gaze.

"You ... look amazing." He handed me a plastic package. "Here."

I glanced down. There was a pure-white calla lily nestled with small sprigs of baby's breath and fresh greenery. I sucked in a deep breath, stunned at my corsage. Maybe he really did love me. "Holy crap, Derek. You did a nice job. This is beautiful." I didn't even know he was going to get me one.

"Glad you like it. I figured you were a 'simple flowers' kind of girl." He took it out of the package and stepped closer to me, his face mere inches from my mine. I closed my eyes and breathed in the light scent of his cologne.

Maybe things were going to be okay tonight, after all.

Concentrating on the task at hand, Derek pinned the flower to my dress. And he did it without even making me bleed. Was there anything he couldn't do?

"Okay, you two." My dad's voice interrupted the moment. "Face me so I can get some shots."

Derek's arm snaked around my back to rest on my hip. I leaned into his warm side. We fit perfectly together. Surely he was realizing it now, even without the benefit of Janet's cupid spell over us.

After about fifty billion more pictures, Mom and Dad finally let us go. Once outside, Derek opened the passenger door of his dark green Ford Focus.

Aw, crap. Something I hadn't banked on was how difficult it would be to get in and out of the car without flashing my goods. After all, this dress was a pretty close fit.

Derek solved the problem by holding out a hand, giving me the leverage to sort of slide my way in. I held on to his hand for a few extra seconds, just to make sure I was in the seat right. A girl couldn't be too careful, you know.

Once he'd popped into the driver's seat, he turned to me and smiled again, melting me into a pile of red-dressed goo.

We took off for the restaurant, making occasional small talk about unimportant stuff. I tried my best to sit as attractively as I could, praying he couldn't see my heart slamming in my chest.

A half hour later Derek pulled his car into a parking spot at P.F. Chang's China Bistro. Which just so happened to be one of my favorite places in the world. Their food was to die for, especially the lettuce wraps.

"Hope this is okay," Derek said. "I love eating here."

"Are you kidding?" I scoffed. "I'd eat here every day if I could afford it." Speaking of, I quickly peeked in my purse to make sure I had enough money. The restaurant had good food, but it was a little on the steep side.

We slipped into our seats. The waiter brought us water and took our orders.

"So, can you believe that about Alec?" I asked Derek a few minutes later, sipping from my glass. Alec was a freshman on my matchmaking list—I'd paired him a couple of weeks ago with Marie, the Hello Kitty girl. The two of them had kept a relatively low profile after being paired up.

Which was why we were all shocked when he'd tagged the side of the school with Marie's name and did a manga-style painting of her face with hearts around it. The principal had been furious, making Alec scrub the graffiti off and then suspending him for two weeks.

"I don't think anyone would have expected him to react so strongly to being matchmade. But Marie had helped him clean the bricks off, which was nice of her." He shook his head, smiling. "The things people do for love, right?"

So very true. I thought about the gorgeous art show portrait Derek had made of me while he was under the love spell. And the crappy leather necklace I'd made for him, now peeking through the collar of his tuxedo shirt. Or those stupid fake eyelashes I'd worn during my disastrous makeover phase.

Our food arrived, and I dug into my plate with gusto. Well, as much gusto as I could while wearing a form-fitting dress. I wondered if it would be tacky to ask Derek to store a doggy bag of the leftovers in the back of his car. Could they make it all evening in the car?

"You know, I'm glad we haven't done anything destructive while dating each other," I finally said, chuckling. "We don't need to get kicked out of school or anything."

Derek widened his eyes in mock nervousness and put his fork down. "Oh. So, you're not into that kind of thing." He paused dramatically. "As a completely unrelated side note, I think we should use the back entrance for prom."

I lifted an eyebrow. "Really? Is there another fun surprise waiting for me?"

He shrugged innocently. "Not anymore, I bet . . . the group of monkeys I trained to perform for you probably escaped the premises. Guess we should have eaten faster."

The rest of dinner went by all too quickly, with us trying to top each other about goofy public declarations of love we could make. When the bill came, Derek swiped it out of my hand. "I got it," he said.

"You don't have to. I have some money."

He laughed. "Mom would choke me if I let you pay. I'd never hear the end of it from her."

I laughed, too, but inside, I was wishing he'd offered to pay because of more romantic reasons. Maybe I was just making things worse with these heightened expectations. Things tended to go easier when I just let go, joked around, and didn't try to read into every word he said or action he did.

The bill settled, we left the restaurant and went to the prom hotel. When I saw the rows of limos pulling up to the front doors, my heart raced. How would things go tonight? Would Derek want to dance with me, or would he hang with his friends and ignore me?

Oh God, I'd be mortified if he ditched me like that. Even though things were going nicely now between us, I feared it could be a different story when his friends were around.

I quickly sent up a silent prayer—*Please, God, if you've ever, ever cared about me, don't let him dump me, tonight of all nights. He doesn't have to be head over heels in love, but don't let him hurt me.*

Derek escorted me to the door, his hand on the small of my back. I could feel his warm fingers through the thin fabric of my dress, and I wanted to turn around and lean against him. It took all the strength I had to keep calm and look normal. Not that I was totally normal in the first place or anything.

"Don't forget," he whispered in my ear, sending shivers across my skin. "Tonight's the night we see who won. Count up your matches, and I'll do the same with mine."

"Hey, man!" Toby, one of Derek's jock friends, said as we entered the front lobby, thumping him hard on the back.

Derek pulled away from me. "Hey," he replied to Toby, slugging him in the arm.

"We have a table in the back. Go sit with us. Catch ya in a bit." He headed off to the bathroom.

I hoped that meant I was invited to sit at the table, too. Otherwise, it was going to be a long night.

Derek and I wrangled our way through the crowd, trying not to trip in the darkened room. The disco light was in full swing, sending dots of white light scattering across the room. The DJ was playing some R & B song in the background, the singer's voice and a deep grooving bass pouring out of the speakers.

We found the table in question and sat in the last two available seats—the rest had jackets draped over the backs.

Derek helped me off with my wrap, then hung his jacket on the back of his seat. "Do you want something to drink?"

"Um, sure. Anything with caffeine is fine."

I sat at the empty table, drawing in deep, relaxing breaths. I couldn't believe how well the night was going so far. Maybe I could finally start to unwind and enjoy the evening.

"—and the cashmere sweater was on sale for dirt cheap," a voice said from behind me. But not just any voice.

I bit my lower lip and rolled my eyes, willing myself to relax. I could get through this. I'd known beforehand I was going to have to deal with her, so I might as well get it over with.

Mallory perched with two of her giggle-box friends in the seats across from me. Goody! "Oh, it's Felicity," she said, her eyes raking over my dress. She sneered slightly, wrinkling her nose. "What are you doing at our table?"

You'd think I'd chosen the seat just to torture her. "Derek's football buddies told us to sit here."

Her jaw tightened for a quick moment. Then she relaxed her face and glanced at her friends. They all rose out of their seats. "See ya," she said to me.

As they walked off, I saw their heads close together. One of the girls peeked back at me, shaking her head.

Great. I just loved being talked about by stupid, snotty girls. Then again, this was no different than any other day. Surprise, surprise—she was one of the unmatched people on my list who I couldn't seem to pair up with anyone.

"Here you go," Derek said at my side, coming out of nowhere. He placed a drink in front of me. "One heavily loaded caffeine drink, at your service."

I gave him a wan smile and took a small sip. "Thanks."

His forehead crunched up. "What's wrong?"

I stared into his eyes, debating whether or not to tell him what a total cow Mallory was. But bad-mouthing her wouldn't make me look any better. "Just waiting for Andy and Maya to arrive."

"I saw them and their dates at a table near the front," he offered.

"Derek!" his friend Toby hollered across the room, waving hard at him.

Derek turned to me. "Hey, let's go hang over there for a few minutes. Then we can go find your friends afterward."

I stood and swallowed, not wanting to go through the whole gig with his buddies yet again. I was still stinging from Mallory's rudeness. "I'll go find Andy and Maya. You can go talk to your buddies, okay?"

Giving him as genuine a smile as I could muster, I turned and left, weaving my way through small clusters of people milling around the room. The dance floor near the DJ was packed with happy couples grooving with each other on the floor, including Adele and Mike, who were getting separated every ten seconds by a teacher for "excessive closeness." As I counted my other matches, I noticed they were mostly couples made by Derek.

Of course they were.

Come on, this isn't the time to be down on yourself, I chided myself. It was prom, and I refused to be a crab ass. Besides, I'd already known going into this evening that I was going to lose the challenge.

I finally found Maya and Andy sitting close to their boyfriends at a table on the corner of the dance floor, smiling and laughing among themselves.

"Hey, guys," I said from behind them.

They both turned around, their eyes bugging out of their heads when they took in my dress.

"Oh my God! You look gorgeous!" Maya cried out, hugging me.

"How is Derek keeping his hands off you?" Andy said, giving me a hug too.

I swallowed, feeling tears of relief sting my eyes. I was so, so lucky to have such great friends. "When did you guys get here?"

"Just a little while ago," Andy said. She wound her arm through Bobby's. "Doesn't he look fantastic?"

Bobby's face turned beet red, and he gave an embarrassed grin, dropping his gaze to his lap.

I smiled, happy to see Andy wasn't holding the car fiasco

against Bobby. Really, it wasn't his fault. "I have to say, he rocks a tux better than you do," I teased Andy, since she has to wear a pseudo–tux at the Burger Butler.

"And Derek looks mighty fine in his, too," Maya said, one eyebrow raised. "How come you're not off swapping spit with him right now?"

My stomach clenched. "Oh, he's talking to his friends," I said casually, waving it off like I wasn't upset by it or anything. "I came over to chill with you guys."

"Need something to drink?" Scott asked Maya. His eyes twinkled in the disco light as he took in her dark plum A-line dress. Not that I could blame him for staring—Maya looked simply gorgeous.

Man, I wished Derek were there, gazing at me the way Scott was at Maya. It was my fault, though, since I'd told him to go.

Maya nodded at Scott with a smile, leaning over and kissing him on the cheek. "Thanks, I'll have a punch."

The R & B song ended, and an upbeat dance number started to play. I glanced around for Derek, hoping he'd remember it was my favorite dance song and come and drag me out onto the floor, especially since he'd put it on that mix playlist for the night of our outdoor picnic. But he was nowhere to be found.

Andy grabbed Maya's hand and tugged her out of her seat. "Okay, we have to dance to this," she proclaimed.

"Come on, Felicity, let's go!" Maya said.

My first impulse was to wave them away and wait for Derek . . . but dammit, this was my prom. I wanted to dance and have fun with my BFFs. I glanced around the ballroom one last time. Still no Derek. He was probably outside or something. Super.

"Okay, let's do this," I said, standing and smoothing my skirt.

We shook our booties for several minutes. My feet started to throb in my shoes, which were totally not made for dancing.

The set of fast songs ended, and a slow song came on. Out of nowhere, Scott and Bobby showed up to claim their dates, wrapping their arms tightly around Maya and Andy.

I stood on the edge of the floor for a minute, watching them and hoping Derek would show up, but my searching gaze couldn't find him at all. Maybe he'd forgotten he had even come to prom with me. Maybe he was talking to his friends about a way to break up with me. A lot could happen in the minutes since we'd gone our separate ways, right?

Maybe the last few molecules of cupid dust had finally evaporated from his system, and now I was history.

Seeing Andy and Maya cuddling with their boyfriends, their eyes glowing with love, was just too much to bear. A surge of tears flooded my eyes, and I left the dance floor and headed right to the bathroom, ducking into the closest stall and sitting on the toilet seat. I grabbed a wad of toilet paper and dabbed my eyes, then blew my nose.

Time to think clearly, rationally.

Honestly.

It seemed to me that right now I was at a crossroads in my life. Everything Absinthia had said was true, and I needed to admit it. I was a failure as a cupid, a failure as a girlfriend, and more important, a failure to myself—after all, the chaos around me had spiraled out of control because of my actions all along the way.

It was time to let go of all of this drama so I could finally move on past this stage in my life. And maybe the sacrifice I needed to start with was Derek. Should I be proactive and break up with him? Or wait for him to break up with me first? Until now, I'd been living in a limbo, waiting for the other shoe to drop. Waiting for him to finally proclaim he didn't want to be with me.

But Derek had proven time and again that he was a good guy and never wanted to hurt people. When I'd accidentally made the whole school fall in love with him, he was never mean to even the most obnoxious of his love-crazed suitors, despite the fact that he wasn't interested in dating them.

I shifted on the lid of the toilet seat. Maybe I'd simply become one of those suitors to him, all gaga and googly eyed whenever he came near. The thought broke my heart into a thousand pieces. But I guess the truth wasn't always easy to face.

I wanted him to love me so completely that he wouldn't let me out of his sight on a night like tonight. So deeply that he'd act like he had during the love spell and not slowly fade away from me as the days wore on and our relationship fizzled out.

Yes, I loved him. Yes, I wanted to be with him. But this wasn't the way I wanted our love to be—initially forced because of a spell Janet had put on us, with him stuck in a relationship because he was too kind to break up with me. And me too scared to ask him for more together time.

No, that wasn't going to cut the love mustard.

I wanted, and needed, more.

I tossed the wad of mascara-covered toilet paper into the tiny trash can attached to the wall. It was time to find Derek and face reality, once and for all.

My hand shook slightly as I pushed the stall door open and walked through. I left the bathroom, broken. Heart in throat, I scoured the ballroom in my search for Derek. I spotted him standing near the punch table with his jock friends and Mallory, whose date was nowhere to be found.

Courage, Felicity. I forced myself to walk over to Derek, who turned to me. His eyes were dark under the overhead light, unreadable. He certainly didn't look happy.

"We need to talk. Privately," I said, throwing a pointed glance toward his entourage. Of all the times in our relationship, now was when I had to put my foot down and insist they stay away.

He nodded. "Yeah, I think you're right."

We made our way through the hotel lobby and stood out front, where there was no foot traffic coming by. A light breeze blew, and I inadvertently shivered.

Derek took off his coat and wrapped it around my shoulders, the warmth from his body heat enveloping me instantly. It was a bittersweet gesture, given that we were about to break up, and I knew this moment would be trapped in my head and heart for a long time.

Crap. How was I supposed to start this? Stupid me, I hadn't thought about what I'd actually say.

"I think it's time for us to clear the air," Derek said slowly. He felt so distant to me, and I knew that with every second passing, he was slipping away from me even more.

I nodded slowly, ready to get the pain over with. "Yeah. Yeah, we do."

Chapter 20

"I just need to know . . . why have you been acting so weird around me?" Derek asked, his voice thick with emotion. "You're blowing hot and cold, and you've been so distant lately. Are you wanting to break up?"

"What?" I exclaimed in shock, heart slamming in my chest. Was he for real? That was not what I'd expected him to say. "Hey, *you're* the one acting all funky, not holding my hand or calling me or being as affectionate with me as you used to. And ditching me at prom to go talk to your friends," I pointed out.

Yeah, he'd only been gone a few minutes, but it still stung, and I wanted him to know that his friends had contributed to the wedge between us.

"I wasn't ditching you for them." He paused. "But I was gone for too long. You're right, and I'm sorry for that." Derek crossed his arms. "I think there's some massive confusion between us. What's going on here, Felicity?"

Drawing in a deep breath, I knew it was time to come clean. "I can tell you're not feeling as close to me anymore since the spell wore off."

Now it was his turn to be shocked. He reeled back, eyes wide. "What? You put a spell on us? Wait, wait—I didn't think that was possible."

"No, it's not," I said, shaking my head. Tears welled to my eyes again, and I blinked rapidly. "The day we . . . became boyfriend and girlfriend, Janet had put a cupid spell on us. Don't you see? That's the reason why you suddenly liked me. And that's why—"My voice broke. I stared at the ground, sucked in a breath, and forced myself to continue. "That's why when the spell wore off, you stopped feeling as strongly for me."

Derek said nothing for a long, painful moment. The only sound I heard was the whooshing of my heartbeat rushing in my ears.

Then he burst into laughter. "Really? You think Janet matchmade us?"

"I don't see why that's funny," I said stiffly, my pride stung by his unexpected humor with the situation. "I'm sure she only meant it to be nice."

"No, no, no," he quickly said, then stepped toward me, pulling me close. He tugged my chin up, locking eyes with mine. "You don't understand. I've been crazy for you for a while . . . a lot longer than two weeks."

I swallowed, a small flutter of hope spreading from my stomach to my limbs. "Really? You have?"

"Absolutely. Janet didn't need to cast a spell to make me love you, Felicity. I loved you, anyway. In fact, I'd told her that right before we started dating." He leaned forward and pressed a soft, gentle kiss on my lips.

Oh my God, I think my heart just burst out of my chest with glee. "You have to know how I feel about you, Derek," I whispered when he lifted his head.

"I do." His eyes were warm, empathetic. "No wonder you've been acting so weird and distant. Carrying around that kind of perception about your relationship could drive a person crazy," he said slowly, shaking his head in wonder. "What caused you to think we were paired up?"

"Um, the day after we started dating and we went to her office, I saw a planner with our names in it. There was a whole list of people, and I guess I assumed those were her matchmaking list." I laughed, feeling a weird mix of ecstatic relief and crazy giddiness, then pressed my cheek against his chest. "Oh my God, this whole situation has been a nightmare. I'm so, so glad that's out in the open now. And even gladder it isn't true."

It was actually embarrassing, thinking about my severe misperception. Derek had been steadfast and open and caring during our relationship, only I'd been too scared and crazy in love to see it at the time. How often had I come across to him as less than unwavering?

All this time I'd been working against my own happiness, keeping Derek at arm's length emotionally for fear of getting my own heart broken. And all this time I'd been hurting him in the process.

I bit my lower lip. Well, he was never going to have to doubt my true feelings again.

We held each other for another long moment, then linked fingers and headed back inside toward our table. I returned the coat he'd lent me, which he then hung over the back of his chair. The first few notes of a love song filled the air, and my heart seemed to bloom in my chest.

"Want to dance?" he asked me.

I nodded, and we made our way to the edge of the dance floor, where there was a smaller crowd, compared to the other side of the dance floor. Derek wrapped his arms tightly around me. I leaned in to him, closing my eyes and smiling blissfully to myself as we swayed in perfect rhythm.

What had started as a sketchy, nerve-wracking prom date had finally turned into the event I'd hoped for—dancing with Derek, the guy of my dreams.

"By the way, I think you won the bet," I admitted. "You have way more matches than I do. I'm prepared to fulfill my end of the bargain, so just pick where you want to eat."

"You don't have to do that," he said. "I'm not gonna hold you to it. But it's nice of you to offer."

"No, I insist." I paused dramatically. "I bet Andy would be happy to hook us up with a great table at The Burger Butler."

A loud laugh jarred me, and I peeked an eye over Derek's shoulder to see what was going on. It was Mallory's date, Doug, horsing around with some of his friends. Off in the distance I saw Mallory standing all alone with her back against the wall, looking forlorn.

Aw, man. As much as I didn't like her, I could totally feel her pain. No one wanted a date they felt was ignoring them. Maybe it was time for me to help Mallory out.

"Derek," I said, "can we go back to the table for just a second? I have a little . . . business to take care of."

He nodded knowingly and led me back to my chair, where I'd hidden my PDA in my purse under my seat. We sat down, and I fired up my good old LoveLine 3000, with Derek watching.

I sent a blank message to Mallory's and Doug's cell phones. "Now watch the magic happen," I said to Derek with a sly smile.

"You're a good person, Felicity." He draped an arm across the back of my chair and rubbed his hand on my shoulder.

"Not as good as I could be," I said, giving him a flirty smile as relished the sensation of his fingers on my bare skin. I turned off my LoveLine 3000 and tucked it back into my purse. "But I'll keep trying."

Mallory jumped a little and dug into her purse, pulling out her cell. She flipped it open and stared for a moment, then blinked rapidly and rubbed her chest.

Bingo.

A moment later Doug did the same. Their eyes met from across the room, and they headed right toward each other. Right in front of all the promgoers, Mallory mashed her mouth against his in a hot, furious kiss.

"Whoa," Derek said, blinking rapidly and jerking back in his chair.

I snorted. "No kidding. I guess she had some pent-up lovin' in her."

After a moment of make-out madness, Doug tore his mouth away and held up a finger for Mallory to wait where she was. Then he dashed madly onto the stage and whispered in the DJ's ear.

The DJ nodded, stopping the song that was playing and turning on the mic. "We have a special request," he said. "So everyone, make sure you have a partner and come out on the floor." Then, he handed the mic to Doug, who cleared his throat and stood ready, lipstick marks all over his mouth, as he stared intently at Mallory.

Derek and I exchanged glances, our eyebrows raised.

"What's this all about?" he asked me.

I shrugged my shoulders. "Hey, I just matched them. I can't control peoples' actions after that." A casual comment, but a lesson I'd learned the truth of all too well.

Derek tugged me out of my chair and led me to the floor again. "Let's get a closer view," he said, mischief dancing in his eyes. "I have a feeling we're about to see something really interesting."

The music started again, a fast groove that instantly got my attention. My jaw dropped. Oh my God, Doug was singing Beyoncé's song "Crazy in Love" to Mallory!

Mallory's friends ran in a giggle-rush toward her, clutching her hands as they all swooned en masse to his serenade.

"Got me lookin' so crazy right now," Doug warbled when he hit the chorus, swaying his upper body left, right, left, right.

His voice was amazingly bad, and we all stood riveted at the sight of his wide-open mouth and vibrating tonsils for a long moment. Even the adult chaperones and teachers were as shocked as we students were, staring at him as he gyrated on the stage.

Mallory, however, didn't care how bad he sounded. "Omigod!" she squealed loudly, clasping her hands to her bright-red cheeks. "That's, like, the most romantic thing ever!"

Derek tucked me against his side, shaking with laughter. I joined him, as did the other promgoers around me.

"It's so sweet!" one girl to the left of me exclaimed. She grabbed her date's hand. "We have to go dance!"

"His voice is horrible," Derek said, still chuckling.

"I know," I said, wiping tears from my eyes, "But what's scarier than his singing is that he actually knows the words to this song! There's no karaoke monitor up there for him to read from!"

He nodded, laughing hard. "This is true."

When the song ended, the entire room burst into thunderous

applause. Doug handed the mic back to the DJ, then jumped off the stage and plowed through the crowd toward Mallory, sweeping her off her feet and spinning her around the room. She squealed again, clinging tightly to his shoulders.

"Let's give one more round of applause to our serenader!" the DJ said, deftly turning on another slow song. "Stay on the floor and have another dance."

Someone bumped an arm into my back. "Sorry," I heard a familiar, throaty female voice say in a distracted manner.

I turned to see what was going on. It was Mrs. Kendel, leading Mr. Bakula, the guidance counselor I'd paired her up with, onto the dance floor. When the music started, she wrapped her thick arms around his skinny neck and tugged his face close to her massive bosom. Their bodies remained locked against each other as they rocked side to side.

With a knowing chuckle, I elbowed Derek in the side. "Check it out," I said, indicating my head toward them. "I finally found true love for Mrs. Kendel."

Derek smiled, then turned to me, his eyes deep, endless. He grabbed my waist and pulled me close. "You are the sweetest, most beautiful girl I've ever seen," he said, bending down to brush my lips with his. "How did I get so lucky?"

A hot flush swept over my cheeks. I kissed him back, then whispered, "I feel lucky, too."

"I'll never forget how beautiful you two looked in your dresses," Maya's mom said to me and Maya on Sunday afternoon. She'd offered to take us out to a late lunch at TGI Fridays as thanks for us helping with her makeover.

Well, Andy had been invited, too, but since she was grounded, she couldn't come. I'd told her I'd throw down some food on her behalf, to which she'd slugged me in the arm and called me a smartass (I guess boys aren't the only ones prone to violence). Sheesh, you just can't win with some people.

"Thanks, Mrs. Takahashi," I said, putting down my menu to check her out. Surprisingly enough, she was wearing one of the new outfits we'd picked out for her. "And thanks again for treating us to dinner. I . . . noticed you're not wearing sweatpants. Does that mean you've given them up?" I asked hopefully.

She laughed, rolling her eyes. "Well, I've decided to wear them only when I'm working out or cleaning around the house."

I nodded. "Fair enough. I'm glad to see you feeling better."

"Me too," Maya interjected. She smiled at her mom. "You look great."

"Thanks. I don't feel completely whole yet," Maya's mom said, "but I'm on my way. While you guys were at prom, I dug up some of my old high school pictures. I was so happy back then. I think it's time to start feeling happy again."

Maya reached across the table and squeezed her mom's hand. "I agree." She shot her mom a mock-serious look. "But I'll have you know there will be guidelines on what kinds of guys you can bring home to date, young lady."

Mrs. Takahashi shot Maya a skeptical look. "Yeah, it'll be a while before we have to worry about that."

The waitress arrived and took our orders. I got a sandwich and soup combo. Yum, I couldn't wait.

Maya's mom took a sip of water. "Your father and I won't be together anymore," she said to her daughter, tears welling up in her eyes, "but we're still going to do the best we can for you."

Maya slid out of her chair and hugged her mom. "I know. I never doubted it for a minute."

"Excuse me, guys," I said, moving out of the booth and into the bathroom. I wanted to give them a moment alone to talk.

And hopefully, start to heal.

Chapter 21

"Rob, I have something to tell you," I said, trying to ignore the vomity feeling in my stomach. I'd put this off for way too long. And he was due to come to Sunday dinner in about an hour. I definitely didn't want him bringing that skank Annette along, faking us all out with her niceness and then getting nasty with other guys behind Rob's back.

"Sure, what's up?"

I cradled the phone between my ear and shoulder, then drew in a deep, steadying breath. "When I'd told you before I saw something happen, I meant something about Annette." Oh God, please don't let him get pissed at me for being the messenger. "Um, when I was meeting her for dinner at Pizza Hut, I, um . . ." I floundered for a moment, then plunged straight ahead. "I saw her kissing Officer Banks."

There was a long, long moment of silence on the phone.

"Hello?" I asked tentatively.

Rob cleared his throat. "I'm here. Thanks for telling me."

"Do you . . . are you mad at me?"

"No," he said quickly. "I just need some time to think. Tell the folks I'm gonna pass on dinner. I'll talk to them later tonight."

My stomach sank, and tears sprang to my eyes. I sniffled. "Rob, I am so, so sorry. I was hoping Annette would be the one for you. I feel horrible." Yet another one of my brilliant matches, gone awry.

He sighed. "Don't be upset, Felicity. It's fine. I know it was hard for you to call me. I gotta go, okay?"

We hung up. I plopped backward across my bed and lay for a few minutes. Poor Rob. I wished I could fix this for him, but it was best if I let him handle his own love life from now on. Hopefully he'd open his eyes and heart to someone more worthy of his time and affection.

Monday evening, at my weekly work meeting, I handed the LoveLine 3000 back to Janet. "I think I'm ready to hang up my wings, so to speak."

She pursed her lips, disappointment clearly etched on her face at my news. "Really? Why?"

I leaned back in the chair across from her desk. "Welllllll, it's because I suck at it. Um, pardon my French. I don't think I'm a natural at the job, like you or Derek. But I do promise to stick to the terms of our contract and not tell anyone about being a cupid. Not that they'd understand it, anyway," I said in a droll voice.

Janet laughed, nodding her head knowingly. "Well, I'm sorry to see you go, but you're always welcome to come back in the future if you want. I thought you were a great cupid, for what it's worth."

"I appreciate that," I said, hoping my sincerity rang through my voice. Even if I knew I wasn't good at the job, it was nice to be treated so well by an employer. "I've really enjoyed working with you."

"Take care of yourself. I'll see you around, Felicity," she said, a mysterious smile on her face.

"Well, in that case, I'll be watching out for you first," I shot back with a wry grin.

"Felicity, can you run this iced tea to table four?" Miranda, the manager of The Burger Butler, handed me the chilled glass.

"Sure thing." As I squeezed past Andy in her butler uniform

behind the counter, I gave her a quick smile, then dashed to the table, my own butler jacket flapping.

Being a waitress who looked like a penguin wasn't the best job ever, but at least I wasn't holding the fate of people's love lives in my hand. Well, not unless I spilled boiling coffee in some guy's lap. Plus, I got to work with my best friend. And the tips weren't so bad, either.

Overall, not a horrible gig, if you didn't count the pervy old men who always sat at my tables.

When I finished handing off the iced tea, Andy tugged me by the arm and pulled me aside. "So, we're still on for studying tonight, right?"

"Absolutely," I said, nodding. "Maya's already promised to come over, and she's even bringing some food."

She sighed. "I wish Bobby could study with us, but with me still being grounded, I figured I wouldn't push my luck."

She and Bobby were going strong. I think it was the longest relationship I'd ever seen her in. Not the two people I would have paired up, but it worked for them. And you know what? Bobby was actually a decent guy, the more I was around him.

Plus, boy, did he care about her. At first I'd almost felt a little miffed that he got over his unrequited crush on me so easily, but since that was petty on my part, I tried to brush those feelings off. He was happy, she was happy, and that's what counted.

Besides, I was getting plenty of ego strokes these days, so who needed a crush to feel good about herself? Derek and I were doing great. Tonight was our six week anniversary of 'fessing up our feelings.

Yes, I was apparently *that* girl, the one who had anniversaries for every event in a relationship—first drink shared, first slow dance, first time swapping spit.

Lucky for me, Derek was a pretty patient guy and dug my quirks.

And also lucky for me, Mallory had totally backed off riding my ass all the time. On Monday after prom, she'd come up to me in the hallway in between classes and had apologized for being so snotty to me recently. She'd claimed it was extreme prom stress, which sounded totally stupid, but whatever. It was the closest I was going to get to a sincere emotion from her, so I'd take it.

Surprisingly enough, she and Doug were still dating, even though the spell had worn off. I guess love had softened her around the corners . . . a much-needed improvement, if you asked me.

"Felicity?" Miranda's soft voice jerked me out of my thoughts. "Wanna clear table nine now?"

"No problem." I grabbed the plastic container to dump the dirty plates into and glanced over at my supervisor.

She was pretty cute—slim body, cute blond hair pulled casually up, friendly smile. She looked to be in her early twenties.

And she was single, too. I'd overheard her talking to another server yesterday evening about it.

Unable to help myself, my mind started churning with the matchmaking possibilities. Even though I was out of "the business," as I'd come to think of it, I hated seeing nice people alone.

A few minutes later I heard the front door open, and my brother strolled in, his beat partner in tow. "Hey," he said to me, waving. "We came to make fun of you while we're on break. Any good doughnuts here?"

I laughed, happy to see Rob wasn't still upset about the Annette issue. He hadn't been around the house much since I'd talked to him about her cheating . . . and when he did stop by, he didn't bring a date or stay long. His only words to our folks on the subject were to let us know he and Annette had broken up.

Mom and Dad hadn't asked what had happened, sensing Rob didn't want to discuss it. Smart peeps, they were.

"You're a dork," I replied back to him, rolling my eyes.

Miranda walked over to Rob. I could see her look him up and down in a quick, sweeping motion. She offered him a small smile and waved her hand toward a booth. "Evening, officers. Would you like to have a seat here?"

My brother looked at her and paused for a moment, then grinned widely. "I certainly would."

Miranda walked away, stopping by me. "Is that your brother?" she whispered.

Well, well, well. Maybe Rob would turn out okay, after all. "Sure is. He's my very *single* brother."

She smiled. "I'll handle his table."

"No problem." I dumped the last glass in my container and walked away, chuckling to myself.

Relationships were a weird thing—some couples needed to be matched up to find each other, like Mallory and Doug, or even Derek and myself. Others, like Miranda and Rob, simply needed the right circumstances.

Love could conquer all, but thank God there were cupids to nudge it in the right direction sometimes.

Acknowledgments

A huge shout-out to the formidable power duo: my agent, Caryn Wiseman, and my editor, Anica Rissi. I don't want to sound too sappy, but you two are totally the wind beneath my wings. These books wouldn't be where they are right now if it weren't for you guys!

I'd also like to thank the rest of the Pulse staff, including Emilia Rhodes, Michael del Rosario, Jennifer Klonsky, Bethany Buck, Andrea Kempfer, Bess Braswell, Venessa Williams, Lucille Rettino, Katherine Devendorf, Brenna Franzitta, Lauren Forte, Cara Petrus, the gifted copy editors, the poor person who had to format all my italics and dashes, and everyone else who's had a hand in the Stupid Cupid trilogy. You guys are seriously the best, and I've loved working with you on this! I'm honored to be published by Simon Pulse.

Of course, I'd be remiss if I didn't say thank you to my incredible family—Bryan, Shelby, Bubs, Pat, Ron, Lisa, Forrest, Lynne, Lou, and Jodi. And, of course, to my extended family too! You've all been so enthusiastic and caring in your support. Thank you.

To all my friends, thank you all so much for your support as well. There are waaaaay too many of you to name, but you know who you are, and I'm winking coyly at you right now.

Lastly, I want to thank you readers for picking up this book. I'm truly blessed to be able to do what I love and share it with you!

About the Author

Rhonda Stapleton started writing a few years ago to appease the voices in her head. She lives in northwest Ohio with her two kids, her manpanion, and their lazy dog. Visit her website at rhondastapleton.com, or drop her a line at rhonda@rhondastapleton.com.

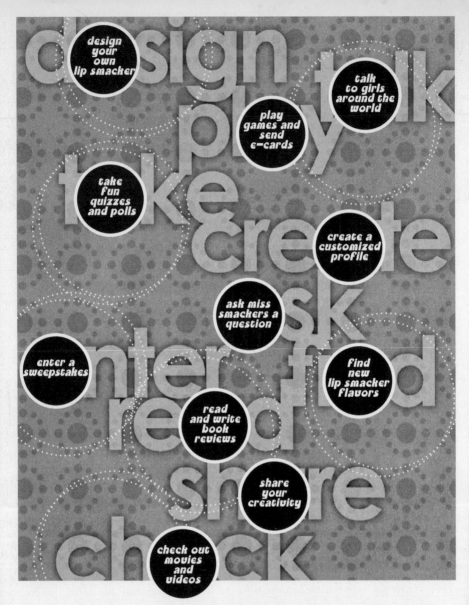

Jammed full of surprises!

LiP SMACKER® LOUNGE

VISIT US AT WWW.LIPSMACKERLOUNGE.COM!